Captivating Passions

Captivating Passions

Matter Iceman

Published by Amorous Ink Publishing
Indianapolis, IN 46218

This is a work of fiction. Names, characters, businesses, places, events and incidents are either the products of the author's imagination or used in a fictitious manner. Any resemblance to actual persons, living or dead, or actual events is purely coincidental.

ISBN 978-0-9883939-4-3

The publisher would appreciate notification where errors occur so that they may be corrected in subsequent printing and/or editions. Please send comments to the publisher by emailing to biz@amorousink.com

Printed in the United States of America

Introduction

I am taking this opportunity to let you know a little about me and welcome you to my inner thoughts so to speak. I began writing to help me cope with the senseless murder of my baby brother a few years ago. A very dear friend of mine helped me by buying me sum notebooks and soon as the pen hit the paper, I have not put it down since. I learned that this talent was birthed out of tragedy in some ways I feel like a phoenix rising from the ashes. That is how I view my writing. I have a unique style to my writing. I call it Hybrid Prose and in a nutshell, it is not a full length story and not really a short story, it is a mixture of the two. Inspiration comes from everything around me, either from situations in my life that caused hurt, love and pain. From others who wish to share their erotic adventures, life altering situations, or just a song popping in my head. Recently I have had some Peppa in my life that has aided in inspiring and spicing up my mind to pour out my soul into every piece I write. I have come up with my Nondaplume. Matter, because I matter to at 3 people them being my kids. Ice, which is one of the 3 stages of matter. And I write in 3 different formats, Erotic, Love and Hurt. Man, is plain and simple to some but hard to others. I man up to handle the responsibilities of being a father and doing the business of a man in the household. I hope you enjoy my introduction in to my Sensual Playground I like to call my mind. So just remember to always live outside the box, never let anyone stop you from reaching your dreams.

<u>*"3 P's"*</u>

Writing from the heart and giving voice to it does it show my intelligence and does it evoke feelings of love.

That passion that burns deep and can make you rise up above.

Above and negativity or hate that shows up to destroy or kill joy.

I come with smiles like that big pitcher of red goodness we grew up on to make u feel sweet.

Busting thru your walls to your heart and then your pussy is on my agenda.

Love to leave you in a state of bliss and pure wonder.

Wonder, woman what will my intellect inspire from you to do with me.

I'm home waiting anxiously to see just what that can be.

Be all we can be to one another.

This story is just beginning for us, all I want is you not any other.

Dropping to my knees to pray that love would find me.

Never lived a life like this, all I can think of is seeing you and getting a sweet kiss.

Solo sang bout Heaven on Earth and I must agree, you are just that, surpassing all your previous worth.

Chasing after you seemed like an impossible dream and I was destined to fail.

Well that hasn't happened like that little engine riding on that rail, I think I can, I know I can.

Because no matter how hard times get I will never bail.

Now it's you that I'm wishing I have all to myself, your love is more priceless than Trump's wealth.

I want you always, and living without your love is no life I want.

Rather much have one that was more eloquent.

Desires to shake you all night long, rock your body from head to toe like your favorite song.

Things you got my mind thinking, just can't wait for all that love we will be making.

Entering the walls and leaving you feeling clear.

Down home country girl or big city chick, this thing we got going on is thick like my black walking stick.

Now like Guy sang, I like, the way I want you, so let's chill, and groove me baby.

Now I know you heard of 3T, but this is 3P, but I hope it feels good, just don't cause the blues, because I don't know what you came to do, but hope my new jack swing gets us to have an anniversary unique between me and you.

"Cleaning it Up"

When you make a mess of things in life it would be great to have some all-purpose solution like bleach to clean the mess. They call on Mr. Clean to get out the tuff stuff. But only bleach can fix this because my life is just that tuff.

Scrub and rub, buff and polish. This life will never be pure and clean. Live and love, doing my best not to be mean. To have a fresh start is crazy but oh I just wish.

Poured out the bottle it has many uses and jobs. Killing germs and making things fresh. That feeling can only be described as one of the best. Used in a pool to make the water clear. I bet sum folk would rather not want to hear.

Why does my life needs to be white out you say. Just some mistakes, that just didn't go my way. White as snow and washed with some good ole chlorine. Some things I'm not proud of because they were just mean.

Now no matter the brand be it Clorox or biz, knock off or brand name. Bleach is bleach no matter what name.

"Rainy Night"

Standing there and seeing you in person were a true dream
come true. I always knew who the great Christina was.
Admiring your beauty from a distance and hoping one day I
could just get one chance with you. Speaking here and
there and never really expressing my intentions to get time
with you. But for some reason the stars were all in
alignment and literally the heavens opened up for this
opportunity to make this fantasy a reality.

 I saw you enter from across the room and instantly knew it
was the angel Christina, finally in living color. I made my
way to you and introduced myself. The hug was good, soft
and I felt like a kid on Christmas morning. I stood next to
you and I felt like I was able to say all I wanted to in the
past but never could. I loved the dress you had on; those
animal prints made me want to unleash my animal on you.
The gold heels you wore just were the icing on the cake and
trust I wanted to lick the icing off your cake.

 Feeling bold and full of energy I just reached out and
grabbed your soft ass, while I whispered to you can you
come with me. Taking you by the hand I snuck off to go to
the balcony. Pressing you against the door, I moved in to
begin kissing your neck as my hands began to travel down
your body to the hem of your dress. Feeling your supple
breast against my chest was sending shockwaves thru me.
Pulling up your skirt I discovered you were going panty
free today. This was also enticing as I slipped my fingers
inside your moist pussy. Just at this time it was as if I
flipped a switch, because not only did you begin to get
wetter, the sky opened and the rain poured down.

Bodies beginning to get soaked, I dropped down to my
knees, placed your leg on my shoulder and went to work

entertaining your clit with my tongue. Licking and sucking intensified as you moaned and pulled my head in closer to the point you was grinding that phat pussy all over my face. As my tongue eagerly kept pace I felt you begin to gush that sweet nectar all over my face I lapped it all up.

 Standing up and turning you to the rail, I told you to grab it and hold on. I pulled out my erect dick and press up inside that wet soaked pussy and I begin slow stroking it. Saying OMG, Christina you feel like heaven and you got me feeling good. Dam this pussy is magnificent. Picking up speed and watching the drops hit your back and ass; I felt it was only right I hit your ass too. SMACK, SMACK, SMACK as I hit and watched your ass shake and the water splashed off. Faster you said, as I obliged you. Harder, deeper I pushed in further. I felt your walls tighten on my dick as I was telling you baby, I'm about to cum.

 You looked back and said good because so am I. Both releasing at the same time as the thunder crashed and lightning streaked the sky. I knew this was a rare event. Both now soaked and dripping wet, that didn't matter because we were fully satisfied. Christina, this was two fantasies that came true this night. Finally I had sex in the rain with the goddess of my dreams. Too bad this was just my dream I had that night after I saw you. However I'm a strong believer that dreams do come true.

"Kiss"

Your kisses are like a burning fire
They are all that I desire

Your eyes are like a calm sea
There is nowhere I'd rather be

Your mind is my main goal
Then I'm after your heart and soul

Dreaming of you in my life always
Want to be in love with you all my days

Searched for this all over
Now this greatness won't ever be over

No games, no lies, no broken promise
Just your hot burning kiss

It will never end with you
This love thing is all I'm ever going to do

"No More"

I no longer want to share what's mine. Nor do I want to borrow what belongs to another. All my life I would just do what I wanted. Now I find myself caught up in an ocean of emotions and no land in sight. Nothing is hopeless and nothing bad lasts forever. But I can't see me sharing for who I'm caring. Caring and not sharing is my new outlook on life. What is mine I want no other to have or hold. Now you're mine and yeah it's bold.

But this feeling is too much from what I was told. But I just know what I want and that is all.

I'm not in love but it could be possible one day to fall. Right now just going slow and seeing where it goes. I'm optimistic and the possibilities are endless. But right now these thoughts of jealousy are making me pissed. Now will it workout, who really knows. But for now I'm falling back and going to regroup. But I don't expect anything from you. Just continue to do you but while you do……

 I'm not going to watch boo. Your voice and mind got me caught up. Well I'm just going to back on up. I'm not like others guys because I'm not going to lie. Just no more and I'm absolutely sure. Now watch as I walk out that door. No more sharing is caring, quote the raven, nevermore. So I'm no one to you but a single friend who wanted a tad bit more. Just seems to me, you're not at all sure. But I know what I'm looking for and it is a tad bit more. Freak, like me and freak like you. We could be perfect being freaks together and doing what two freaks do. I handle that, accept that and want that. Guess I'm not worthy like others to receive that. Making sweet love is my major passion or fucking like rabbits is outrageous fun. All I want is to be the only one, Hun.

"Shared Passion"

I like the way you did that. Standing back watching you plow into her, I began to feel the passion and intensity she was feeling. Remembering the last time when I was in her position. We were getting it in only like two married folk should. Feeling your tongue explore every inch of my body as it finally reaches its final destination between my luscious thighs. You said get comfortable, we are about to do something unusual. We are going to try every position possible.

Reaching up and feeling your head bounce up and down, I tried my best to hold back my spontaneous expressions but you were working like you was teaching my clit some pleasure lessons. Baby please work that magic that u do oh so well. Feeling this fire swelling up inside me I knew I couldn't hold it back much longer. Then pulling your head in closer, forcing more pressure to be put on my clit, I asked you to slide in two fingers.

 Just as they pierced my opening, I was too threw; I released such a moan as I squirt out my sweet nectar all over your face and hand. That didn't stop you though, because you continued. Saying girl I didn't know you could get down like that. As you kept going I began to squirm more as the sensations were magnified due to that beautiful orgasmic release before. Legs aching to close and arms flailing, you did a swift move to lock me down. I was no good as you stayed there and I was at your oral mercy.

Finally raising up and informing me it was my turn to exhibit your tools from your wheel house. I pulled out your dick and said excuse me have I seen you before, as I smiled with my big brown eyes. All at once I engulfed you. Sliding up and down your shaft as my mouth got wetter, I pulled up and used my tongue to trace that one vein from the base to the tip and back down. This time I began to suck and play with your balls with my tongue. I tried my best to fit them both in my mouth at the same damn time. Taking my hand and stroking your muscle while I was getting acquainted with your balls. Moving back to the object of my attention, I realized it was a little dry so I spit on the top of it and entering my mouth again I tried to race the drool to the base. Reaching down you held my head and said yes baby, I'm going to fuck your face tonight. Almost gagging a few times, I took every inch of you.

Looking down our eyes met, this just intensified my motion to move at a more vigorous pace. Twisting my tongue around and sucking like a vacuum, I could feel you getting hard and reaching the point of explosion. You pulled my head up and said hell no, I'm going to cum on that ass tonight. You picked me up and told me to get on all fours. Coming in behind me you leaned down spit on my ass as it trickled down to my pussy, you smacked my ass, said here comes daddy and you pressed all that meat into my wet pussy. Slowly at first till I said give it to me like I was your little bitch. You sped up and as I began to throw this entire ass back on you. Piston was pounding and I could feel that thickness spreading me open more and more. You said baby your pussy is heading for self-destruction.

I knew that once you said that the pussy was purring and I felt the orgasms hitting back to back as I was screaming yes daddy, oh shit daddy. I'm cummin daddy. Damn this dick is good. Face buried in the bed and my ass just being pulverized, I felt you do that little stutter stroke. I knew that meant you were about to cum. So you pulled out and I said put that shit all on my ass. I reached back to spread my ass then I shook it as that love cream started to slide down my ass. Damn I watched as you was taking her like you took me. And I stood there as I felt myself getting wetter as each stroke went in and out of her pussy. At that moment her date came up to me and started to kiss my neck and move his hands up and down my breast causing my nipples to get even harder. Hell they were hard from me playing with them as I watched you. He then moved me to the bed next to you and his girl. Spreading my legs he saw that my pussy was already soaking and dripping. That was just an invitation for his tongue, as he began to lick and lap at my clit. This was feeling oh so good. However normally when we come to these events I usually only get my pussy ate, but on rare occasions I want to feel some penetration.

I do this because normally I only cum with my husband but watching him, I knew once that dick was inside me I would cum like a fucking waterfall. So I tapped him on the head and said please fuck me. He was all too happy to oblige. He pulled out his condom and I reached back to stroke it a bit while he opened the wrapper. I mean it felt thick, but it wasn't my baby, but I know it will serve the point for this occasion. He slides on the condom and I put my face down and ass up as he pressed in me. And it was thick and he did what I wanted. He went slow and fast at different times till I came on his dick. Looking over and seeing my wife watching I knew how she enjoyed seeing me fuck another woman. So I did just that.

We started out with me and her going downstairs to the playroom; my wife had followed us but stood back on the wall. I sat the little cutie on the edge of the bed and she pulled at my shorts, pulling out my dick and she began to slow stroke it with her hands. She looked up and said to my wife, do I have your permission to play with your dick. My wife said feel free, suck and fuck that shit my dear. She did just that, she sucked it like it was the last hard toy in the world. She sucked, slurped and gave her tongue a little twist all over me. I felt my knees starting to get a little shaky. She said she can't stop and she won't stop. Meaning my wife said that. Sorry this head play is messing me up mentally. But damn, and whoa she just wouldn't let my dick go. She said she got you daddy. And I was like hell yeah she does. But I got the final word here. So I backed up and said no, you not going to get me till I get you. So I pushed her to the bed, spread them thighs open. She said be my guest as she spreads open the lips. I sucked that woman's soul out of her as I got a hold of that clit. Taking my hands and squeezing her nipples as I traveled up from her slit to her clit with my tongue.

I played around the hole while fucking her pussy with my tongue. She began begging to get fucked. I said no I'm not ready yet. Told you I'm in control here. I reached up and pressed her legs to her chest and I literally went in head first into her pussy. She screamed and moaned as she began cumming so hard. My wife stood back with her hand rubbing her nipples and the other massaging her pussy. I said ok, now I'm ready. She leaned forward to stroke and kisses my dick while I got the condom out. She took it and placed it in her mouth. She then put the condom on me by using her mouth. Said damn haven't had that since I was in college. Told my wife, baby, you got to try that. She laughed and said ok.

So my sexy lady turned over and said, enter when you ready. I smacked that ass and said let's get it. Pushing in deep, I felt that wetness surround my unit. I sped up and said damn I like this. Long stroking was what I was doing and then slamming in harder. I said sorry for party rocking as I started to rock the shit out that pussy. Pressing down on the small of her back to get that arch, I leaned up to put all me in her. She moved that booty like she was an ocean wave. My dick felt each orgasmic wave as she came. Next thing I look over and my wife is getting dicked down. Seeing her cum made me cum as I envisioned that it was me blowing her back out. Next thing I know, shorty did this booty pop and I just released. Damn, what the fuck you do as I pulled out. We got up, thanked our play partners and walked together to the bathroom to clean up. Both us smiling hard and feeling very pleased. I said that is why sharing is caring.

"Love Juice"

Sitting here just imagining how good it would be to come in behind and gently place my hands on your hips. Slide my hands up your sides to your shoulders at the same time I begin to lean in and kiss your neck. I pay close attention to the spot I found on my last trip when I explored your sensual spots. You know just in the corner where your neck meets your shoulder. I part my lips so slightly and just every so smoothly glide my tongue over this spot. I can feel your body begin to have slight tremors. Taking my hands now and I turn you around to lock eyes so I can show you the passion that is beginning to ignite in them. Pulling you close and feeling your ample chest pressed against mine I move in close to give the longest and most sensual kiss.

With the kiss you know I mean the one in the movies where it is in slow motion. Lips coming together in a meet and greet that is only spoke in love stories throughout the ages. With lips pressed and slightly opened so that our tongues begin to have a gentle wrestling match in our mouths. Our hearts begin to beat as one single heart beat moving in such precision as the beat of a drum line in that championship marching band.

My hands begin to go on the exploration of the rest of your body moving down to caress your soft booty and this causes my mind and my body to respond to you and you begin to send a surge of sexual energy throughout my body that causes my muscle to begin to rise. I could only imagine how your passion is swelling up and beginning to flow in that most inner part of your womanhood. I move to your ear and whisper to you that baby this is just the beginning I plan on drinking every drop of you and becoming INTOXICATED in your love juices.

After I leave from your ear and gently nibbling it as I begin to use my tongue to trace the intricate details of every curve of your body moving down slowly to admire the rest of your body. I move you to the bed and begin to slowly undress you and meticulously pay attention to every hot zone of your body. I remove your bra and pull one strap down and expose a beautiful semi hard nipple just staring at me begging for me to attach my lips to it. So I do just that and as I do, I feel your body shake with a beautiful tremor as if to say finally. I then slide the other strap down and begin to take my lips over to the other nipple as to make this matching pair not feel neglected in any way.

Once removing your bra I begin to move down to your waist taking my hands and unfastening your pants and as I pull them down your curvaceous body and expose the creamy caramel thighs I just imagine in my head how juicy that you're becoming. I pull off your beautiful green boy shorts and I stop to say baby I love how u match and you know green is my favorite color. I start down below at your perfectly pedicure toes and I wrap my mouth around each toe and begin to weave an elegant trail from your toes up your legs remembering that spot I found just behind your knee.

Then moving my hands up your thighs and as they continue to move up to give your breast a massage fit for royalty. I take my tongue and mouth and make my move toward your luscious brown sugar honey spot. I take my tongue and start to lick your clit gently and slowly making sure I am getting every drop of love juice that is just flowing like a waterfall. I move my tongue in circles and up and down as if I am painting a masterpiece as fine as the Mona Lisa with my tongue. Making sure I get every inch of you on my canvass. I move my tongue as to insert it inside you repeatedly and with gentle precision I find myself lost in

the moment. I hear you moan in joy and ecstasy as you tell
me baby please don't stop I feel myself about to explode.
So I do as I am told, along with you holding my head and
pulling me into you more I use this pressure to apply more
vigorous movements of my tongue on your clit until I feel
your body quake like a 9.5 earthquake. And I open my
mouth as to do like I said earlier to drink every drop of
your love juices.

Feeling the joy swelling up inside I just want to plunge
myself deep into your love tunnel. I rise up from the sweet
center of your thighs. Blissful and excited from drinking
from u and tasting your juice, I know now I want you to
feel the power of my love and energy at its full force. I take
my muscle that you have caused to become stronger and
harder than a diamond and they say Diamonds are a girl's
best friend. So baby get ready for your best friend to come
visit you and go deep inside to the inner parts and release
the full power of the energy that has swelled up inside me
since I first laid my eyes you.

Taking you from the bed to press your body to the wall and
standing behind you I take myself and enter you from the
back as I feel your body shake and quiver as if you just
melted in my arms, I proceed with slow and easy strokes as
my hands cup and caress your ample breast. Grinding and
moving in sync to that special love song we play in our
minds, our bodies become one. Turning you around and
staring deep into our eyes I can see that your fire is only
beginning to ignite, so baby lets set this wild fire free.

Taking you to the bed and sitting on the edge I pull u on top
of me with your legs straddled around me I fill you up with
all my power and passion. With long sweet deep wet kisses,
I whisper to you that baby this is the best day of my life.
But now baby, it's time to get down to business. I stand up

and turn you to the bed, with your back on the bed and legs wrapped around me I begin to press deeper and with more force. I feel you getting wetter and juicier as the stiffing of my tool start to glide in and out with the constricting of your walls I tell you "oh baby you know exactly what I like." Feeling the pressure build up inside of me, I am like wow; I just can't believe you have me about to explode. Baby you are going to be filled up with all the power I have. I want to release the passion you stirred up in me from when I first place my first finger to your exquisite frame. I think it's about time I use my dick to write my name the name of the man that mapped your body. That man that use his oral skills to open the flood gates and release your sweet juices. Now that man that entered your tunnel and tore down your walls and filled you with pure joy and passion. "Baby I am cummin, Oh yes I am cummin, hell yes you just made me cum so good!" Damn you are good. Now wait till tomorrow when we can do this all over again.

"Bold"

Oh it was just my IMAGINATION was a borrowed line but when it comes to expressing my intentions to you, they are 100 & true blue.

 Beauty like yours is unique, rare and hard to find.

Was there any doubt I am making this PLEDGE to make you all mine.

I desire to be your king and treat you like my queen.

More regal and ROYAL than those that comes from England.

 Just face it I'm your biggest cheerleader, hell I'm your number one fan.

 Now as I part from this little poem about your beauty. Cherishing you, loving and respecting you is my honor, pleasure and most humble duty. So what is stopping you? PATIENCE is not my forte' and nor is COMMUNICATION. But I do know that those need to be PRESENT, if I want a FUTURE, and not a repeat of the PAST. Had a talk with the MAN in the mirror and I am making a CHANGE. Traveling thru life we come across a lot that we tend to ALLOW in our lives that bring good and bad. I'm not sure how or why there has to be, but good and happy just always accompany sad. They say joy comes with the breaking of dawn meaning a brand new day. But when pain is this bad there is not much good you can say. However, when you come across something that brings you joy attempts to take away the pain.

Just the one to RESUSCITATE your life brings back the sun that dries all your rain. Don't give up the hope that you deserve to be happy, just ACCEPT the goodness and love that is shown. It comes from place that is very well known. The heart I have is big and strong and mighty as can be. I'm happy to show you the best part of me So no longer DISCREET. Love is to be shared and fully exposed. Not hid and in secret, hell that bullshit just blows. So why do we have to keep our love hid behind closed doors. Let it flourish and grow, like the HAPPINESS we both come to know. No one values the love like I do for you. But as long as I'm open and upfront my LOYALTY to you is never in doubt. Now step in my life and spice it up like CINNAMON.

Sprinkle the love and turn up the sensations of joy in my world. You send my mind to new orbits and with you by my side I know I can do anything. You are my strength that helps me pick me up when I fall face first in the DIRT. You show me my true worth and I do the same. This is joy and what we have is love without any game. This might seem a tad bit lame but I promise to always treat you extremely fair. Your beauty, smile and love got me soaring high in the AIR. Now when this piece is all said done, just realize you are my loving one. But just in case, this was also done to show I'm 100% true to you. I'm focused only on one, which is what this was all about.

<u>Wanna/Gotta</u>

Beauty is unmatched,
Flawless design,
Body being watched,
Just stay on my mind.

Wanna get with you! Gotta get with you!

Chasing after what you got,
Going all in for you,
Stay making things extra hot,
I know your worth and true value.

Wanna get with you! Gotta get with you!

Dimensions on brick house status,
Heart is in love mode,
Bringing that kick like a fruit with citrus,
Got me so ready to explode…

Wanna get with you! Gotta get with you!

Can't wait much longer,
Need you now and then,
These feelings just get stronger,
With you I'm always going to win.

Wanna get with you! Gotta get with you!

So let's get together,
Make our lives with each other,
Just know things can't get any better,
Just so much for us to discover….

Wanna get with you! Gotta get with you!

So you ready to get with me,
My love is yours and it's totally free.

<u>"Rhyme Time"</u>

I have strained my mind trying to find a way to spit something easy as pie.

I just want to step to you correct and bring my A game, like the tat says.

Now I'm bringing the truth like I did from the jump and that isn't a lie.

To have, hold, honor, respect and stay 100% loyal to you is my pledge.

This may be funny to some folk but I'm tired of dreaming of you from my bed.

Thoughts of you passing thru my mind left and right

If it was anyone else, I would wish I could keep you out my head.

Since its you, I plan to make this work and using all might

Now pop goes the weasel and pop goes sum people's dream of being with me.

I would love to show all the interested parties a great individual time.

There are many and many lovely beauties as far as I can see.

Check it out; I'm here to say I'm not that easy, can you share my time.

I plan to slip in your mind and bring forth all dreams and plans.

So with no question I begin to pull forth all the love too.

My final goal is to go shop for some ass wedding bands.

Making you fall in love with me is all I'm inspired to do.

Now while others sit and wonder what has transpired?

And others just get mad, and then look for cracks in our foundation.

Too bad it isn't that easy because our passion and intensity burn like a wildfire.

So as far as anyone's problem is, we the only two in our love nation

Lips soft as cotton and eyes deep as an ocean

Now if you ready, let's get it on.

That heart you have and love you share was your special love potion.

With you I know is the right and only place I really and ultimately belong.

<h1 align="center"><u>"One"</u></h1>

I will be the one who will love you like no one before

The one who will deliver passion on the regular and pair it with intensity

The one who will take you anywhere you want to go

The one who will never hurt you and will always protect you

The one who doesn't make a promise that he can't keep

The one who will be there forever because you satisfy my every desire and need

The one who will stand by you and cheer you on

The one who will tell you the truth always

The one who avenges your pain, hurt and loss to make you smile forever

The one who will give you more than anyone did before

The one you can trust with your love, mind and body

The one who accepts all the flaws because I know we are only human

The one you can cry to and laugh with

The one that is for you

The one to give you endless nights to remember

The one that will shower you with endless kisses

The one that will build his world around you

I'm the one, not number two, so it's, always going to be just
me and you.

"The Ride"

Leaving the club it was bout 4a.m and I had just got off from doing security. I was asked by one of the bartenders for a ride home. Now let me say Meek, was one fine woman. She was tall and just thick in all the right places. She was an Amazon type and she could mix a mean drink. I would watch her shake up a drink and the way her body would move shook me up. The short black skirt and long sexy legs was all I was seeing while she sat next to me in the car. Every time I saw her I would just wonder how it would be to start from her sexy toes, licking and sucking each one as to make each one feel special. That crazy design you had them looked good as they peeped out thru your shoes.

Moving up those legs, long and luscious that led to sum thick and juicy caramel thighs. I knew I just imagined how they would feel with my lips on them and even still with my head between them. Licking my lips, I think Meek caught me starring and she saw the look of insatiable and animalistic intentions in my eyes. I say that because she slid her skirt up more to show her green and white thong. Then she took my hand and placed it right on her pussy. She then slid the thong to the side so that my hand had an unobstructed path to her sweet spot. Meek, really baby as she then guided my fingers to slip inside her. It was warm and moist and I could feel the wetness increasing, as she applied more force to my fingers. Her body was squirming in that seat and as my dick was hard as a rock.

"Meek, you wet as shit baby."
" I know keep going, don't stop, please don't stop. I'm going to cum, yes, oh dam yes, your fingers feel so good."

"Oh baby, I'm cumming."
 As Meek let out a huge sigh of passion, she then took her
hands and began to pull my hardy boy out from its hiding
place. Taking her hands and double fisting my dick she
stroked up and down for a bit. Next thing I noticed her head
went down and my dick disappeared in her mouth. Slurps
and sloshes began to become the sounds that filled the car.

"Meek, OMG, what are you doing, you are doing, hell I
can't think right now."

 Just trying to stay focused on the driving became
increasingly more challenging because Meek was working
the hell out of my stick shift. Down she went, back up
again, my mind was all over the place, luckily my driving
wasn't and I was glad because the cops were out. Meek,
hope you ready for what I'm about to serve you. Pulling up
you said," yes baby unleash it all in mouth."

 I did just as commanded. Right then, I just let go and
released all my cream in that warm tunnel of her mouth.
We then pulled up to Meek's house. She asked me to come
in but I regretfully declined. She asked for a rain check and
I happily accepted.

"Rain check"

After my last encounter with Meek, I was thinking what I could do to cash in my rain check. What I decided to do was call her up and prepare a surprise for her. I asked if she would be available to go out. Meek replied yes and we agreed upon a time that I would come pick her up. I also told Meek to be dressed nice because we were going on a real date. Arriving to her place, I knocked on the door and Meek came out with this beautiful dress on. It was semi-long, although she looked divalicious in it, I love looking at her long sexy legs. Anyway, Meek you are the definitive definition of beauty personified. After our last encounter, I haven't been able to get you off my mind. So we got in the whip and made our way to Zenga for Chinese. Pulled up to the valet and I escorted her inside. Watching as you walked up the stairs ahead of me and your ass bounced so beautifully like a perfect picture.

Sitting down to dinner I was in awe of your beauty. And I knew I wanted to seduce this woman. I dropped my fork on the floor so I bent down to just look at them legs. I thought when I get home she is going to love this surprise. We had great conversation from the election to how we are both pleasers. After dinner, we walked the streets of Chinatown for a bit before returning to get the car.
 Looking over and asking Meek, "can I cash in that rain check?"
She said, "How you are going to do it?"
"I can show you better than tell you."

 We then pulled up to my place and again I escorted inside. I took her to the bedroom and we began to undress one another then moved our party to the shower. Washing and soaping each other down caused things to heat up. Hands caressing and moving around passing underneath her breast, grazing your nipples, I brushed against you and my dick became harder. Stepping from the shower we dried each other off and then Meek moved to the bed as I requested. I lit candles and burned incense to set the mood for a sensual full body massage. Beginning with the feet a firm but gentle feet rub. Firmly moving up the legs bypassing any known an erogenous zone, Meek was in total relaxation.

Now my mind switched from seducer to freak and I spread her thighs of goodness open and I proceeded to explore her vision of loveliness. I stuck my tongue so far into her she thought it felt like my dick inside her. Grabbing and holding her thighs I pressed in deeper, tongue massaging everything from the clit that was stiff to the lips hiding her womanhood. I felt her cum and leak out onto my face. She moaned me to stop however I just kept at it. She began cumming and cumming too many times to keep track of. Rising from the bed, and standing there hard as a brick, I said Meek, now I'm a true pleaser and that tongue lashing you just got is all we are doing tonight. This rain check was all about pleasing you.

The Message

Sitting in this meeting just bored to death, listening to the boss talk about something about the end of the year business. But all you could hear is blah, blah, blah. Then out of the blue, your phone which was set to vibrate starts to go off in your lap where you had placed it. It was me, texting you the itinerary for the evening when you got home from work. Now it was the start of my weekend, yeah on a Wednesday. This was the hindrance to our sex life, the weird work schedules, but I was going to try to correct it tonight. So with these 160 characters, you picked up and read this.

"Come home, take off all your clothes and join me in the shower. Wash off the day and rinse off the stress. Then prepare to get even hotter and much dirtier"

Replying back you said "baby stop, I'm in a meeting and I can't talk." So I sent this.

"I want to caress you from behind, as the soap and water runs down our bodies. Then turn you around to drink the passion from your full thick lips so gently"

"Baby, please, I'm begging you to stop. I can't focus. You have my mind wandering and heart starting to race." So not stopping I sent this.

"Moving from the shower still dripping wet, I told you to lie on the satin sheets. Slide them thighs apart, you bout to be dried off from my oral heat as I eat"

Moisture level now reaching its apex, mind just now stuck on getting home to me for some hot passionate sex. One more from me came through though.

"Let me suck your stiff nipples, caress your plump breast. Part them thick thighs with my hard thick prize all the way in you as I get lost deep in your eyes"

That was it; the LAST reply just said damn that felt good, I just had to excuse myself to the bathroom where I pulled out my lil friend B.O.B. to aid in my stress relief. Tried to be quiet, but I didn't however that is another story. Well, just waiting for you at home baby in the mood to use all my sensual moves.

Mentally Hijacked

It was just a normal day; the sun was out and shinning with
the birds tweeting. Dressed on my way to work, so I get on
the train and this is where I believe it happened, where my
mind was mentally hijacked. Now I had met this beautiful
gift to humanity a few weeks ago on this same train. She
wore this beautiful yellow dress, with a sort of black half
sweater and some sexy wedges, but what caught my
attention was that sexy tattoo just above her ankle.
Normally I'm not that shy, but today something came over
and I was just hit with a bunch of nervousness like never
before. Although, in my observation of her, I noticed there
was no ring, so that fact helped calm my nerves, but what
really calmed them was the way she smiled at me when she
say me checking her out. She looked at me and said take a
picture, it will last longer. However she didn't do or say it
in a rude way, but it was more of a flirtatious joking one.
Oh baby, I just love to admire beauty and I'm just doing
that because you are exceptionally beautiful. I know our
time on here is limited but if you would bless me with your
phone number, I would consider a great honor and pleasure.
So my nerves were gone, because she said all that to me. I
felt strangely weird at first, but in a good way. She told me
I was handsome and she was about to get off and she
wanted to continue talking, so being the type to please a
woman, I happily gave her my number. This new
generation of independency still shocks me, but being the
forward thinker I am, I can adapt. After a nice handshake,
we parted ways. So around lunch time, I got a call, and it
was her, we talked like we had known each other for years
all the way through our hour lunch break. Needless to say
we planned a date, and it was terrific, been on about 3 since
then and each one was better than the last. So as I am on
this train today, I started to get these messages from her, but
they weren't any words they were all just pictures, nothing

nude, just her in a sexy purple and black outfit in different poses. This woman set my mind in fire, I mean the thoughts raged in my mind and not even Smokey the Bear could have warned me about this. I mean she was looking so luscious and juicy; hell Perdue would have been jealous. The thing was she knew I was a visual guy; I get more turned on when I can use my imagination to picture you in my mind. Nudes do a little for me, just cause I am a true blue red blooded guy, but leave me some mystery. Let me undress you mentally then when we are together I can do it physically. Images came to my phone for the 30 minutes straight, because that was how long my commute on the train was. Once I got off the train, and tried to call her back, all my attempts were sent straight to voicemail. Thinking something was wrong at first, until she text me to tell me that she just wanted me to think of her today and wait till I could see her later to give my thoughts on what she sent in person. Well I stopped calling and replied back that I understood. Well that was it, she stayed on my mind all day like a tattoo, and she permanently was plastered to my mind all day too. I had a hard time trying to focus at work, thinking about when I see her tonight and what possibly could happen. Watching the clock all day, like a kid in school waiting for the 3pm bell. Once I got off I couldn't get home to wash off the day fast enough so I could change to get over her place, because she was cooking my favorite meal, meatloaf. Once there she opened the door, I was greeted by her in a green dress and sexy heels, a kiss and a hug. I told her I was waiting patiently all day to come home to you. Then I told her thinking of her all day, was beautiful, exciting and extremely romantic. You had me mentally hijacked all day; everything I did just brought my mind back to you. Now I'm here, so let me show you what I was thinking about.

Physical Escape

After a delightful meal, and telling her about her pictures that morning had me wondering about her all day. She asked what was I thinking, I looked into her eyes and grabbed her by the shoulders, she said baby boy this your moment, so what are you going to do about it. Pulled her in close to begin a deep, passionate kiss that sent sparks flying as it was a fireworks show. Not sure what happened next, she took over I believe, biting my bottom lip took me by surprise but it was not a turn off, more like a turn up. Now she pushed me back only to let me know that this night she was taking full advantage of me. While she was sending those pictures, she herself was getting turned on thinking of what could be possible after dinner. She basically told me she wanted a physical escape with me. I knew this chick looked amazing, felt even better and I was digging her vibe about being in total control. She took my hand walked me up the stairs to this room that contained a huge bed. I stepped in and she informed me that to enter into her realm of pleasure I had to remove all instruments that would bring distraction to the appointed task at hand. Removing each article of clothing at a smooth pace, I didn't want to seem too eager now. She just pulled the straps down and step toed out of her dress, however she left them sexy ass heels on though. Follow me to the bed was the next instruction; she crawled up in the bed, and then motioned me to treat her body as dessert and to go down and taste her moist cake. Her body felt so smooth like freshly spun silk. Stroking her legs gently, kissing up her legs, to nibble on her inner thigh, just to arrive at my aforementioned destination where I had been booked at to perform. Suddenly her hand came down on my head and pushed me straight into her. She told me the hell with the slow soft shit, I been waiting for the lips to be sucking this clit all day. Hmmm, shocked at first, I was, but that pussy tasted like straight honey so this worker bee did what the queen asked. Licking and licking, sucking after suck, even stroked her with two fingers till she exclaimed to put more fingers inside her. Thinking damn, this pussy is getting extra wet now. How that pussy tasted, oh damn you better make that kitty purr. Especially if think you gonna be inside her with that tool of yours. This woman I'm thinking is unlike any other, and to get that river to flow from this well was a struggle. Man come on; treat this pussy like it's yours for one night only. I was sucking that clit, flicking my tongue on it slowly and making circles, man you doing that shit now, her back arched, moans came pass her lips, oh shit, that is right, baby keep doing that right there. Wow, you putting my mind in a zone, that's right, baby now bring momma home, speed up, I like it, oh yes, yes, yes, and here it comes, oh hell yeah. Legs started to shake, as her river just ran and flowed all over my face. Boy you better drink my juice if you expecting me to inhale everything from your phat blunt you got. I got stupid wasted off her love juice. Now she said lay down on the bed, and if I touch her then the show is over and I must gather up all my clothes and go downstairs and sleep on the couch. But if I follow all her orders then tonight she will be fucking me with all her might. Now bring that dick to me, you have an RSVP with my mouth that must be kept.

Final Sensation

I took full control of this situation like she was destined to do so. I should have known that she was that type, I mean she did flip the script and asked me for my number. She took my dick like a true pro. I mean baby took her mouth and made a cocoon and sucked it so well, that I thought a butterfly would emerge. Her head game was so tight, hell she belonged in the hall of fame. Up and down, slurping and sucking, then rolling her tongue around the head. Not a big fan of this but she was truly making me a believer. I was fighting all the urges to grab the back of her head, due to the rules being expressed from the onset of her oral demonstration. She was going so fierce on my manhood I couldn't hold back the release of my power all down her throat. As she took her lips away, she told me I better not release because I was not given permission. Damn near begging, I told her you so good, I can't help it. Well you better learn today to have dick control. Dreaming of her all day hoping she would unlock all the sensations that my body could handle. Mind went blank as my eyes rolled to the back of my head, next thing I knew, she was on top of me in a reverse cowgirl position. Rocking back and forth, side to side then up and down as her ass bounced. Right there right in front of me, almost begging me to grab it and slam it hard back on my waiting dick. She knew what she was doing to, turning back saying I dare you to grab this phat ass and see what happens. Clinching my hands and digging into the bed, I just let her have full control. This is my prerogative, I'm going to do what I want, now do I have a problem with it? Again, bout to have the damn break she told me, remember the rules permission was not given. So the thought of football raced through my mind. Success, the urge was subsided again. Back down to give me that fire top, until she climbed on me again this time face first so I could see them beautiful breast bounce just out of reach of my mouth. Torture that is all I could say. She leaned over, breast just inches from my mouth, she asked if I would love to bend her over and smack this ass, then explode all over it. I smiled and ridiculously shouted yes, yes, yes. She said ok, then got up only to go back to give me that unforgettable oral pleasure, then just as she pulled up a bit, she said permission granted. I immediately shot out all that special lubricant. And she took every ounce of it, nothing passed out of her phat lips. The final sensation indeed, she finally allowed me to touch her as we hugged and fell into each arms in the bed. Baby you really turned me out, you were my thrilla in Manila, and I love a take charge woman. Suddenly, I woke up to my alarm going, breathing was labored and body covered in sweat. Damn what a truly realistic dream that was. After getting dressed, I made my way to work. Got on the train and saw the exact woman from my dreams in the same yellow dress. Wow, was this some freaky Deja Vu', or was this a preview of what may and could happen.

Cinnamon Twist

The mood is set for an exciting adventure something I never thought would never had happened to me in all my life. Who would have thought this lady would ever find such joy and passion from another that turned out to be the same as me. Being a mother of 2 grown children and working my way through a painful divorce it was time for me to get out there and let my proverbial freak flag fly so to speak. Now I can say that I had experimented earlier in life with many different sexual escapades such as the foursome and then with another female before marriage but nothing too serious, and all that was fine, sensational and exciting filled but after this recent adventure my mind is fully blown wide open and my passion is set to overload status. It all begins on my little vacation to do one of my favorite activities, that being line-dancing, yes you heard me correctly line-dancing. Well, let me share about one of my fun filled nights from this weekend. Since January, I have been seeing this female on a serious, real type relationship. I had invited her to my special trip being that she does not live in the area so this was our first time seeing each other in a quite a while. The nights we shared were so magical and passionate. Being with another woman is quite a special and sensual event. She touched and teased every inch of my body along with my mind, She kissed my neck and caressed my shoulders, cupped my breast all while holding this intense eye contact. Parting my thighs and delivering a cascade of sensations that lead me to have gorgeous revelations about this new combination that may not fit the normal regulations but she had my body composition reaching sum new higher elevations of pure bliss as she was delivering some erotic and passionate stimulation. She used her toys on me and just let me truly have it. She treated me special unlike any other had before, She showed patience and concern to ensure that my satisfaction was reached each night we were together. Rising and rising, feels like the river is about to overflow with a rushing and gushing trying to get out. Feeling as though a treadmill is the ground upon all is walked. Rather ran, the rat race that pushes all and if you can't handle then those will fall. Pressure begging to be released, with no outlet to be seen what to do when the force is ready to explode like never before seen. Will you help with the stress, although I can't promise there won't be a mess! Beginning to feel the ground swell of energy from down below heart racing and chest pounding needing to find that switch, in which she was the key to the itch. It was because of her one touch or many touches, her one glance that took me to this overload status. I can't stop wishing, won't stop missing, that fantasy trying to be a reality I'm hoping for. Touched, waiting to be desired and only she could do it. You're the only one that can ease the beast, calm the storm and make my body feel oh so warm. Satisfied by your body, eased by your kiss damn, baby this was all I ever wish. Just made me happy passion abounds and your body was touched and pleased all around. Now as I lay here in my bed all I can think of is just thoughts of you. The way you make me feel and the way you just carry that certain swag that just turns me on. Well that was borrowed from MJ, but I put a twist of me on it. Now I remember a time long ago when late nights consisted of dreaming and wishing, hoping and praying, for something nice to enter into my world. Well my lonely days are gone yes and I still pray but now I pray for us pretty baby. You cause a good kind of sickness to enter my body and affect my mind. Love sick is that condition and that is just no fiction. You caused me to get an addiction to that wonderful friction. You caught me off guard and made me pursue you with reckless abandon and without regret or regard. Regard for fear, confusion or anything of the negative sorts. I just want to work to keep you satisfied. Love crept in and now I'm up

all hours of the night thinking of you and not tired in sorts.
Ladies come in all shapes and sizes. And you fit every
desire and fantasy. I aspire to make you my one and only.
Wishing that you could be here just a whole lot longer, but
just know the time away makes these feelings grow a little
bit stronger. To hold you down is my dream and to have
you hold me down makes us a team. They say it's a first
time for everything and you are a true first for me. Nothing
typical or average, just the person I need you to be. I
finally picked the right one and just like that search, this
piece is done.

Case Study

When you step back and take look at what makes you happy, have you thought maybe love, pain and heartbreak could be better understood if it was a case study done about it. Look at dating, going out doing things with a person that allows each to get to know one another. Making slight micro decisions on how they will fit into the preconceived life models that you have. Now no one is saying they want to domesticate anyone it's just that we have dreams that everyone wants to come true. So no cookie cutter mold can really hold what I expect from my partner. In search of a mind that has been liberated and set free to roam and join mine in explorations. So being one that is not afraid to lock hearts, let me explain to you what a case study relationship is. Not being the type that thought one night adventures would be in my destiny, I found that if you take time, watch previous interactions and just put selfish needs on the warmer there will be a new dream built that will be strong and then all fantasies would be made reality. When one learns it's more important to focus on the affection rather than the erection, then the study will head in a great direction. Everything is based on perception with a clear interpretation you can see life with no deception or false speculation. Learning to be funny and spontaneous can take one very far. Treat them with respect always and hold them to the standards that are held at a high bar. Be a friend that leads to a lover and let love bloom, blossom and flourish so no one can come in to disrupt your end results of the study. I arrived to the choice to take on this endeavor because I was ready to settle down with one, just got tired of only being a buddy. Our passion that comes from two, that have created a strong mental and physical bond. Think I have one that will fit my parameters and of whom I'm really digging on. One glance by her makes my heart skip, jump and play double-dutch. Just knows how to keep her diva style in just the right dose, it's never too much. Thoughts of her run thru my mind, so her mind I long and linger to also touch. Treat your woman with the same respect you would treat your mother, not that one is looking for a replacement just someone who loves one another. This is my study, so stay off my case I'm the only one who can unwrap her gifts, peel back all the layers and mend the broken and shattered. Because until you can see a woman as a deep open, a blooming onion and a special present from above, then you're just not ready for something that will really mattered. But I'm here, ready to change, I hope after this, I leave you totally flattered.

Disrespectful Sex

Come in, take off your clothes and get your sexy ass against the fucking wall. Looking into your eyes and I tell you this shit bout to get unbelievably real, no love making or sensual ass bull shit. This is about to be sum straight disrespectful fucking sex. Strong kisses placed on your neck, biting followed by heavy breathing on your part as I grabbed your breast with a force that was slightly painful but not too unbearable that had you biting your lip to stop the moaning. Pulling your hand down to feel me growing through my shorts you better hold that dick, and get ready, because I'm putting it everywhere that I want to and you will like it. Daddy, yes, put it anywhere slipped out your mouth through the moans of pleasure. Moving you by the hand I say get in the bed on your back and spread those legs. Taking my hands to spread you open wider, I take my head down there, where I nibbled in each thigh as I made way to insert my tongue first to moisten that increasingly growing clit so I could slide one finger in. Oh yeah, as I slurp and stroke you slow, only to speed up and as I do that I add more fingers till I'm fucking you with all four fingers. Do you feel that, this is my pussy and I'm just getting you opened up for this thick ass dick that is gonna stroke you till you beg me to stop! Faster and faster I went, with more pressure till you said please fuck me, I want that dick in me now. All I said was shut up, this my pussy and I will decide when I will fuck it, not you! Now turn your ass over, ass raised up, I smacked it harder a few times, telling you to never talk back to me. Now, you wanted this dick right, well too bad you going to get this fucking tongue once more. I licked all over that pussy and around that asshole only to be hit with more begging for dick. I even bit that phat ass of her a few times, just enough that I left a perfect dental impression without breaking the skin. Smack! As I hit that ass again this time, I got up, walked over to the side of the bed, with my dick semi-hard, I said suck it and if you good, I may consider fucking you. Grabbing the back of your head, I made sure you bobbed back and forth on my wood. Wrapped my hand with your hair as I made sure you took all of me. I could feel the pre-nut leaking out. Oh chick if you drop anything, then no dick for you. I snatched her back, pulled her ass around to me and said here. I pushed my entire dick inside her, and she couldn't handle it all at once she screamed a bit, that it was too much. Shut the fuck up, you asked for it so you better fucking take it. Oh shit, that pussy was soaking wet. I knew she was creaming all on me. Hmmm, I could feel the pulsations quicken and she knew it, she was throwing that ass back on me. My knees were starting to buckle a bit as I said stop, what the fuck you doing. She said you shut the fuck up, this dick, my dick fitting to come because I fucking want it to come. So mutha fucka come on this phat ass now. Moments from exploding, I pulled out, positioned myself so I could see her face, as I said fuck this and I released my whole clip on her face and mouth. As I stroked out the last remnants, I stepped back and said don't ever try to take control in this room, cause I will disrespect your sexy ass each and every time.

Broken Ice

When you first meet someone it customary to have some sort of introduction, a way to get to know them, well most instances that is called and ice breaker. Well how about I speak on a series of events that crushed that, maybe one could say the ice was broken after this encounter. Well just another day chilling around the way, when a beautiful creature was spied by my little eye. Looking like she just stepped out of a dream, body dimensions were something that just grabbed attention. So walking up and asked, "what was your status, because baby, you look like you the baddest." Started to have you laugh out loud and snicker like I was a king of comedy. Just could not keep my eyes off of all I could see. Thinking if it was possible we have to somehow create a U.N.I.T.Y. Soon after a brief time, it was now time to part company but them digits had been captured just in the nick of time before the doors on the train closed. However as the doors closed, I knew from that brief interaction, this story was about to be blown wide open. After a few hours had passed the phone rang and it was my call from heaven just as I knew it would. Now they sang you can't play with a Yo-Yo, but I made my intentions up front that I was trying to play in her playground and dig in her sandbox. Never the one to brag or boast, but I knew I wanted to rock her body like her favorite dj. My skills so tight that she would flow like the mighty Mississippi if I had my way. Well that call sparked more curiosity and set the mind into motion, so much that she informed me that the conversation was starting to heat her up. Not sure how that was happening, I mean all I did was mention one of my fantasies. How it would be to have sex on the subway. And that one was brought up because of the place we met. Well maybe it was how I said it's all about the mind capturing then the body pleasing. Whispering sweet comments that would aid in the minds ensnarement just doing all it took to please the mind's eye, exposing it to a stimulation that stayed true to course with no deviation. Suddenly a sigh came across the phone followed by a sensual moan; I immediately knew she was showing herself some personal attention. It was all about that self-loving and affection. Not going to front, she was causing me to get an erection. Let her know that her body was superb and it deserves to have all my attention. Tell me more was what I heard next as her breathing hastened. Feeling herself like T-Boz, all I could say was just imagine it was my finger just stirring your pot, turning up the heat by adding two, then three fingers all to make you extra hot. Like any good chef, they have to taste their product, so replacing the fingers; my tongue went in to aid in the reduction of the horniness. Think about hands creeping up north, blazing a trail toward the mighty mountains you call breast. Circling until the tip top is reached only to be pinched softly and massaged firmly. Oh baby yes, when can this happen, as she moaned out in excitement. Damn, that was off the hook. Well after that, plans were arranged to meet the next day for what she thought was going to be a simple massage. Too bad she won't see that was all part of the mirage'. That grand diva was going to be my mine and she doesn't know what was in store for her. Now that's how you really break the ice.

Crushed Ice

She took a trip over to my spot expecting that massage, but my mind had something else in store for her. Had big plans for her, wanted to be buried deep in her soul, swimming throughout her and causing her to spill that sweet nectar from her honeypot until I was finished and felt she was fully empty. Walking in and sitting on the edge of the bed, I knew it was only a matter of time before I maneuvered myself between her thighs, just to talk and lock our eyes. Not sure what happened next, if it was the fact I truly desired to sensually seduce her well put together body which she had in that brown skirt. Or could it be that sexy ink perfectly placed on that thick thigh. Hmmm, it just may be the combination of the two to be honest. Thigh ink is a huge weakness for me, right up there with some sexy sandals or heels. Well back to the subject at hand, inching my hands up them thighs and reaching the Promised Land only to find out she has a secret, that she is going commando today. Just thinking you letting that baby breathe huh? Only thing on my mind was giving that massage, a seductive tongue massage to that most sweet of inner places. After putting up a little fight, she finally gave in and she immediately felt like this was just right, what she really needed this night. Once I pushed through, I let her know Resistance was Futile, now let me have my evening snack. My mouth was in candy land, sucking all I could and moving my tongue in all the cardinal directions, going north to south, then east to west. Damn baby you do that the best. Moved from the south as I walked my kisses up her body, reached her chest and that was were mouth decided to stay and rest. Attention to every centimeter was the purpose set out from the time she stepped in the door. Looking good from the first time, this woman truly had no idea what she had in store. She gave full warning that she was a squirter and that just intensified my oral movements once I returned to the Deep South with my watering mouth. Back and forth I went numerous times followed by sucking and licking that let her no option but to pour out that sweet juice in my mouth. From there, the next move was to press my thickness into her pearly gate. Moving in like that was my house because it felt so warm; I really thought I was home. Once inside, she couldn't hold it back, she blew up again and again and then some more after that. Now this wasn't a problem at all so I just slow stroked it more, until I pulled them legs in close, she was sitting Indian style against my chest. From there I treated her like a drum and beat out a symphonic harmony as she was hitting all the high notes. Orgasms fell from her mind and body like she had no control. The sweat mixed with passion covered us both like a blanket. Just as I thought it was my time to shine, so I pulled back out and bent her over to start the process of getting mine. I said to myself I had to feel that entire ass thrown back at me. Hell she took it all; she literally crushed the ice with her moves. She was popping and dropping, twisting and grinding so well I felt like I was in a blender. Busting out all over that phatty felt down right sensational. She fell face first to the bed and I had to brace myself for a sec. She said I touched her in all the places. And I did, I had to make sure I hit all her bases. As we both rode this high, it was soon time to say bye. But as the plot thickens, this story is only beginning. Don't predict any type of upcoming ending.

Fantasy

What do you think if I want to?

Lay you down on my bed,
Massage you from head to toe,
Use my hands to explore every inch of you
Kiss each spot as I leave it for another
Oh the way you feel beneath my fingertips is amazing
Touches that leave you in quite awe
Wanting to slide your legs apart and place my hands
between them
Take my tongue and ravage your well till it leaks in my
mouth and drenches my face
Turning you over and placing you on your knees so that I
can taste your nectar from another angle
Arch your back so I can see your chest rise and nipple poke
out
Stand up behind and have you face me so I can introduce
you to my manhood
Wrapping your hands around it and swallowing it all whole
slowly
Feel my hands grasp the back of your head to help control
the flow and stroke
Pull back and tell you "No" I want to be inside you
Lie down on the bed and let me make love to your body
Crawling toward you while you spread open your thighs
Taking each leg and placing on my shoulders to press deep
inside
Feeling the wetness draw me inside and feel your muscles
clamp down
Pull back slow and push back in repeatedly as we move in
sync
Dropping one leg to the side as I press deeper and lift up on
your ass to more depth
Feeling you release on my dick we switch positions that

now you are on top of me as I lay on my back
Dropping down on me and grinding to that slow beat like a
classic love song
Raising my hips up to take control of you while pulling
your legs forward to have all access
How about we just move to the edge of the bed and you
straddle me
Take your legs and wrap them around and move in a
horizontal motion several times
While my mouth becomes well acquainted with your breast
and nipples
Hands dig into my skin as you are about to release yet
again
Force that sensation from your body and let me have it
drench my tool.
Stand up, turn around and drop you to the bed so that I can
place my head in that well again
Take my lips and acting as a cocoon to suck on that clitoris
as you drain more into my mouth.
One last moment I desire to be in you, as you get on all
fours and turn that ass to me
I swell up and enter you one last time with a force and a
passion like never before.
Gripping your hips while you throw that ass back on me,
matching stroke for stroke
You giving blow for blow and as the speed increases, you
feel me start to shake and quiver
You moan out in a loud outburst and I just release with
such emotion like a bullet from a gun
Empty clip and empty holster are what we have left.
Falling into each other's arms and breathing at a quickened
pace
This is just what I fantasize about when it comes to you.
Just one fantasy of me, can we act it out, it's all up to you.

.

Inspired Flavor

There stands a Queen, draped in her royal PURPLE.
Looking like a trillion dollars. Frame so majestic that all
the men and sum women just want to scream, shout, and
even holler. Unmatched by any that came before. No
wonder we all just sit back and quietly look and adore.
BEAUTIFUL some may call her, and I am one to agree
fully.

This creature from heaven is nothing short of an Angel
truly and absolutely. Thus from here on out, it is
IMPERATIVE that I obtain her grace, her favor and that
much sought after attention. Because from day one I was
hooked on her damn her with that unshakeable attraction a
GODDESS among all others. I knew she had to have a rack
of lovers.

She was standing there looking extra sexy in her black lace
outfit with some LEATHER accents at well placed places.
Damn when she walks in a room, you can only imagine the
looks on everyone's faces. THICK are the thighs and legs
that get me caught up each and every time!

I swear this BEAUTIFUL woman just stays running around
my mind. Sweet as a CUPCAKE, I can't begin to explain
my immense craving to devour your sweet PINK
womanhood. Everything in and on you just looks so damn
good. Sweeter than sugar that leaves me stuck, like I'm
swimming in CARAMEL.

 The look you gave from the across the room had my mind
feeling oh so well. Nothing like this had ever happened to
me before. She had me running, chasing and looking, damn

I was just craving for more and more. LOVE is powerful and the attraction to you is just as strong. Too bad these thoughts I am having, some just might think it's too early and deem them wrong. However it's my life so imma live it my way. My new mission now is to capture your mind so I can taste your lovely STRAWBERRY between the thighs that are so thick as cream. Well, this is it the end of my lovely dream, too bad I couldn't connect to make us that winning team.

Accepted

She KNEW that there was something about me that she was drawing her in. EVERYTHING was leading her to chase and pursue her curiosity. NEVER thought it was possible just from a single glance that I gave her. DARE to try and figure out if my heart was as big as my eyes and just as warm.

READY to take the chance to see what happens. ALL signs pointed to yes that taking the opportunity to know me would be well worth it, so she allowed me in and I her, had me wondering if I would ever let anyone in again. With all this love to share, it is hard to find someone to trust. I may not be the one to hold a conversation at every second and writing out my feelings comes easier than they are spoken.

I was thinking that I want to open up and share my world; however that leaves me open to hurt, pain and misfortune. To hell with that this time, they say love is good for the soul, and I really want to find one, so together we can grow old. Too many fake so called friends running around. All of which makes my hope meter steadily go down, down, down.

It's hard with all the thoughts running through my head to explain how I feel. I'm sorry it's difficult to pour out all this because it's been kept under lock, key and seal. Case by case is said to be the easiest way so past pain is not passed on. But too many times by just being me I get passed on by. So to you that want to KNOW EVERYTHING NEEDED DONE RIGHT AWAY to gain full access, just give me some time, I will open up fully, and not all may be perfect.

 Just promise me, that all me will be compassionately accepted. So let's go and share, pick up the phone when I call, I want to see that you really care. Now this is it and that is all.

Chess

Knight takes Queen that is the goal of this match. No rush just patience and careful thought to make the right moves. No pressure to move like in checkers, you jump around and move quickly. Apply that to the pursuit of the opposite sex and see how far you get. Again when you move at a hastened pace you will only end up being crowned king. Now that might be all you care about is making yourself the top spot and can do anything you like and go anywhere that is pleasing. However, when you slow down, make choices that will aid in the pursuit of a partner one will see a greater reward.

Something that will be beneficial to both not just one, now some bad choices may get made just look at them as pawns. They are the bad choices and mistakes that get made along the way. One step at a time move by move think of the future not the here and now only. That is because the future is what one hopes for. Life has to be lived like a chess game being played by an Origami master.

Allows things to unfold in due time. So in conclusion, patience wins all the time. No need to rush, rush, jumping here and there for self, when in time the Knight can capture the Queen, totally mind and body. Together they can move in any direction with each other.

Secret Crush

I never lived my days like this, the Lord has gifted me with such a wonderful thing and that being my imagination. I walk around with a smile on my face because it is you that has taken full control of my mind taking liberties with my thoughts that were unimaginable. The only thing is that you don't even know I have a secret crush on you. Thinking of you every time I see an image of you or you just walk by in person sends my thoughts to a level never thought possible.

Yeah, I know you belong to another and just the kind of person I am won't allow me to cross that line to take from another. Karma is real and I am not ready for its wrath of cruelty. Every little step I make the image of you is there. Now before you think this is just some ole stalker type bs let me tell you that you will not see me jumping out of bushes. Nor will see me peeping in windows, and in this day and time, not even social media stalking is a part of my agenda.

So it is just down to this guy finding you unbelievably attractive in mind and body. Just thinking how to get you hooked on me is a constant thought, but not an obsessive one. The idea of being your man is one that intrigues me and thinking how every waking moment we are together, I could explore different avenues of pleasure and joyous sensations. We talk on the regular and I listen to everything that passes through those full juicy lips. Every joy every pain the ups and downs of your everyday life.

 Sometimes I just want to wrap you up in my arms and make every negative thing just turn to a positive. Been thinking about these feelings for quite some time, and each time I'm around, you send chills up and down my spine each and every time. Those images of you dance in my head, the words you speak swim through my soul and the time we spend together makes me wonder is this how heaven would feel. But you know what all this is only the fantasies of a man stuck in the friend zone, cursed to be here because due to age and the fear of losing a great friend. So I will sit here and keep all these feelings to myself and watch as you go off with that guy. This is just the life of a secret crush that exists in a life full of moments.

"Issue"

You know I miss you and the issue is that I can't kiss you. I don't think I can handle this much longer. The urge to be with you is getting stronger. I just want to be pressed between your thighs with my tool. Baby I just aim to be your love making fool. Imma treat you ever and oh so good. Being your man I should. Not would of or could of but would you and could you and could you handle this wood I carry for you. But I have every confidence you know what to do.

Before this goes deeper than I plan for it to. I just want to say how much I miss you. You and the lips so soft like cotton. Your thighs thicka than a snicka. Booty so soft I call u pillow top. Cuz I can just go to sleep on it. Your beauty grows infinitely bit by bit. I relish being in your company. You know by your side, walking as equals, dam that is one sight I can't wait to see. You're my gift from above. No wonder why I fell in love.

Sensuality is a fantasy for some. For us it's a key part of our reality outcome building a castle of love here and in sky. Leaving drama and hate behind as we wave bye. But we say hello as we build our love. Steadily as we rise and rise high up above. Now love can take you many places of joy and bliss. Who would have thought we would be here off just that one first kiss. But I needed your mind first in order to be mine. You were and are the rarest of finds.

"Father"

Back in the days I sit and wish I was a kid again. That was when things were simpler. Well being raised by my grandparents I was able to get a, strong foundation and have my roots strongly planted in the Lord and church. I had my mother who was there to ensure I knew that was there. Always remembering those talks and lectures because I used to have to give an accurate accounting of what was learned and discussed. Those three were there to aid in my growth, development and helped shaped my personality and moral values.

Well I can't to talk about the other half of my DNA, that being my father. Now I can't say I had the best of relationships with my dad but I do know my father was a good man and a great dad to my brothers and sisters. Now he is an even prouder grandfather. Didn't really know all details to why my parents weren't together. I know the stories but as I grow older, I have reached out to get a stronger bond with my dad. My father is a strong man and has worked to have an even stronger character.

 I realize everyone in this life makes mistakes, to quote my dearest friend's favorite songs we are only human. So I forgave my father and I went to talk to him. And I learned a lot of things I didn't know which I'm glad I know now. I'm glad he is my dad and that I am his son. Despite all the tragedy that has befallen our family recently he is the rock in my life. Now I can't say it's not taking work on both sides but I know when I call on my dad he is there.

I hope to be like that with my kids. Their mom and I aren't together and like my dad, I missed a lot of things in their little lives but I have worked to change that and I am here now and forever. No matter a father has a duty to the best man and first man in a daughter's life to show what a real man does for a woman he, loves. Thus he is also the man that shows his son the duties of how real man treats his woman and family. Father, pray for me and my family and thru all I know you are there and for that I love you dad.

"Lady"

There was a song some years ago called "Treat her like a
Lady", and this song had the women feeling like they was
the best things walking. Somehow, that has kind of
disappeared. Well I want to say that in this microwave
society I'm looking for that lady again. I want to tell you
I'm not the ordinary guy u dealt with before deeper than an
ocean and heart bigger than the Grand Canyon. I have put
focus on u because I just want a real woman and friend who
know how to be a lady and can be a freak with me also.
Just want blunt honesty and if u give it so will I. I want you
to know you are a beautiful person to be desired and
feigned after. I want to be one of those guys that see you
thru all veils and masks. Past all representatives and sees
your great big heart. I believe it's because I'm a kuntry boy
and I was taught to be respectful to ladies. I to this day am
proud that my mother and grandmother raised me and my
grandfather was my male role model the guy that will open
the door and give you a compliment just to brighten your
day. I walk on the outside when walking down the street. I
just think women should be viewed and respected in a
certain way and held to a certain standard. Like a shining
star high above in the sky, I stand back and admire the
beauty and awesomeness you deliver to me and the world.
Your beauty cannot be matched by any earthly creation.
Your fashioned by GOD himself to shine for him and with
that I am just happy to be granted just a moment in time to
experience the joy u provide. Yes I know I must share your
beauty with others but I am glad

Melting Ice

Let's try this one more time, never been one to take defeat,
denial or rejection as the final answer like on that game
show. From the very start it was your BEAUTY that caught
my attention. Seeing you on a consistent basis when you
drop by the gym to get your workout on I would step to you
now and then. Always knew I could coax a laugh and a
smile out of you. This went on for a year, never would get a
meal, not even a cup of coffee, hell even meeting up for a
drink during happy hour somewhere was out the question
too. So what is a person to do? Feeling like this ice wall of
yours would never melt.

Then one day, not sure how it happened, but after an
intense workout, I stopped you by the showers and tried
once more. Now I had made up in my mind that this would
be the absolute last time I would ask. Persistence I hear is
sexy, but obsession is not. So I asked, low and behold, I got
that elusive and eluding yes. So I received the number and
we parted ways. Did not want to seem too anxious so I
called later that evening round 9p.m we talked, she laughed
and it was like talking to a best friend, there was no dead
air between us, hell next thing I knew it was midnight.
Damn baby, we just talked up a storm. Before we hung up,
we made plans for our first official date. Only thing I asked
was for her to wear a Raspberry beret' when we go out.
Sounding confused, she said hesitantly yes. I informed her
it would all be explained when we go out.

 Finally the date night was upon us, went over to pick her
up from her house. Oh that dress she had on was dynamic,
long on one side and came up to expose a most delicious
looking thigh. Felt like I was Perdue the way I was visually

inspecting them legs and thighs. Let her know just how impressed I was with the body she works so hard on and how phenomenal she looked tonight. Oh and she honored the humble request with that beret'. So I told her get ready, we were going to an open mic spoken word event and it was a special theme night. She asked what the theme was. So I said it was Prince Night. All the artists had to perform pieces incorporating his body of work. So I informed her that I wanted to use her as my inspiration so I wanted you to wear the beret', so when I see you in the crowd, I can get more inspiration, from that and your beauty.

So once it was my turn, I set up a chair in the middle of the stage and asked you to come. Reluctantly, you made your way down to the front, but not without some gentle urging from the audience. So you take your seat. Informing the audience that you were my date and I asked her to wear the beret' to add to the affect. Stepping up to you and whispering would you mind me being your diamond and let me explore your pearl. STIMULATION of your mind is the key; I have no plan to do you any harm. Would you let me kiss you like it was 1999 in your spot where your cream flows? May I use my tongue on your BREAST first, only to aid in the MANIPULATION of your senses, to leave you ready to call out my name? Have you feeling like my darling Nikki writing songs and poems about you all the time. Feeling your body against mine is feeling and a sensation that MONEY can't buy.

Walking around you and just imagining how sexy would be lying on your back and letting me steal the nectar from your well. Placing soft TENDER kisses to each of your inner thighs as I slowly pull them apart then quickly close them to say no, too early, this is not the easy way. Knowing your mind is my target, building a bond with my essence to tie into yours is what some may call LOVE. I look at you deep into your eyes, licking my lips hoping to get some of you, only if it's a few luscious sips from between your sexy full hips. Now as I stand here looking at you, feeling the heat begin to rise from that SPICY look in your eyes, it may be time to end this poem. So baby, I used Prince to rule your mind so can you be the Princess that I make mine.

As the crowd clapped and applauded my little piece of free speak. You got up and allowed me to escort you back to your seat. After the event was concluded, we mingled for a bit then our exit was made. Back in the car you let me know how you were kind of shocked; tad embarrassed but totally turned on. Dropping you off back at your house walked you to the door where we kissed for a bit and oh yes that was it.

Back in the car, I just thought I melted that ice with my fire. Then I got a text not even up the street yet saying, that she was so inspired and she loved being desired and it had not happened in the longest time. Would I come back and please reignite my fire. Turned around and went back, walked up to an open door and went in. What happened next, well that is another story.
You allowed me to just admire you. You are that true Lady.

Black Ice

Walk in and close the door was a tad bit FEARFUL at first. True the night was superb and she seemed to really love the surprise date we went on. However this was her HOME, the place where her FAMILY roams. She exclaimed from the back to have a seat on the couch and she would be right out. Looking around and admiring the decor, when she walked in wearing this sexy outfit, see through top, sexy sheer skirt and some delicious looking heels. Oh to top it off, she still had on that raspberry beret'. Standing there looking like a true vision of loveliness, she told me she loved the show and my words caused a reaction in her mind that sent the chain reaction throughout the rest of her body.

She stood there looking at me with a sort of hunger like she was going to devour me. She asked me to play a game with her, so I asked what that would be. She smiled, looked at me asked me had I ever been in a situation where I was not in control. Thinking to myself what does she have in store? So I said I have but not in a long time. I would like to again though, just haven't found anyone strong enough to capture my mind to make me want to relinquish control. Well she said it's going to be a night that you will not forget, just like you got my mind earlier, I'm getting yours now.

From my many failed attempts to date her before she knew that I was a visual person. She played this game where we had to say a sentence and the other had to come up with another that rhymed and made sense still. Thinking back in my MEMORY, I knew I could win because I played this game with friends in college. Well needless to say, I let her win, because my lyric game is tight. But you know at times, you take one for the team. So I lost, so I had to strip naked and agree to do anything she wanted.

So once naked, I followed her to the bedroom. Found myself tied down to the bed, hands and ankles. Feeling like I had no control, she came back to stand over while she peeled off her outfit right in front of me. Normally I would feel like a kid at Christmas UN wrapping my gifts but this time she did this SENSUAL strip tease. Dropping each piece to the ground so that the only thing left was the heels and the beret'. She crawled up my body like a lioness on the prowl. She was licking and stroking my body with her tongue then her fingertips, she moved her body up on mine kissing and caressing my chest. Purposely she bypassed my manhood as it was growing and starting to throb. She was seducing me like she said she would.

This woman pulled out all the stops; she began to pour warm sweet smelling oil over my body where a sensual massage promptly ensued. Moving up my chest and down around my shoulders, then up to my neck to return back to my chest. Sliding back, I could feel her ass, and it felt soft and plump, rubbing up against my erection. My mind started to race as my heart was pounding in my chest; this woman had the softest touch but still firm enough to get the full appreciation of this massage. She knew exactly what it took to get me to that point.

Now usually my ENDURANCE was long standing, but I couldn't take any more of her teasing my body, so I was begging her to get inside. I wanted to feel her. Hell I knew she was just as turned on because I could see it in her eyes as she was grinding back and forth on my body as she rubbed my body. Finally she got up and made her way to my manhood, she took one hand and proceeded to stroke it up and down, saying hmmm, this is really thick. I felt it against my ass, and I was curious to see it and now that I do, I'm very happy and now let's make each other satisfied. She moved over to position her mouth on my manhood and she began to move up and down, long slow movements devouring me whole, I swear her tongue was twisting around and spinning as she came to the top and went back down. Speeding up, moving faster and furious, she did some shake and bake move that sent my eyes to the back of my head. Made my toes curl and my body rose up as I exploded like that volcano in Italy.

Like a true diva, she took all me down her throat. She released me from my restraints and asked did I like not having control. It was different, but enjoyable. You know truly captured my mind and took my body to satisfaction. Just like black ice sneaks up in you the night and causes things to happen. You just snuck up on my mind and caused all kinds of pleasure. This was worth the wait and I'm ready for what comes next. And she said with a mischievous grin, I come next.

Ice Cubed

After dropping my guard and allowing you to take full control over me, it now was time for me to show you the full extent of my capabilities. Show you why I'm DETERMINED to make pleasuring your mind my main focus. So now I must please your body. So yes, I heard your slick comment, and yes you will cum, cum a lot. Let me take your body that paradise I dreamed of, the one untouched by man, and have faith in me, that your satisfaction and pleasure are my sole focus. Moving to the shower where the water runs, not to diminish the flames of passion that are burning, but only to ignite them further.

Locked in a sensual embrace lips meeting and melding like two objects just drawn together as if magnetic force was involved while tongues played back and forth like a sensual wrestling match was taking place. The water was hitting us my hands traced behind every drop that was running down your back. Finally breaking the lip lock, I had to press you to the shower door and made my way down your body, leaving a trail of kisses in my wake as my path was leading me to that Promised Land down south. Taking your thigh and resting it on my shoulder as my tongue began a second match with your clit this time.

DELICIOUS in its taste as my full bodied tongue made sensual gestures toward it. Like a new sunshine breaking through, that was how that sensation began to break throughout your soaked body. Water running down your body mixing with your natural liquid made this shower scene an epic tale. Although this was just the first stage of this FLAMBOYANT sexcapade, that was over a year in the making. What is going on in your mind is what I'm asking. As we moved from the shower to the waiting bed, it was only the RECIPROCAL and right thing to do was return that deep, firm and gentle massage to her body. Suddenly I motioned her to raise her firm ass in the air as I pulled out my full thick SNAKE rose up to make its way into your warm waiting tunnel of joy. Slow and steady the course was laid out. Slow in and slow back out, feeling her moan in such pleasure just made me want to speed up little more.

Knowing she was getting caught up in my web of desire, as I had started from her mind, then to her body and as each stroke pierced her more and more, I spoke to her telling her how good she feels, rubbing on her ass and caressing her back with my fingertips, damn I felt like I was playing grand piano the way I was tickling them sounds out of her. Changing positions, she wanted to ride me and feel my hands move across her chest again, so only too happy to oblige, she was on me and. I was sucking, stroking nipples up and down only to put them in my mouth as often as I could. Her hips jumped, jerked and grinded all over my manhood. Just thinking to myself how this shit feels so damn good.

Her KNOWLEDGE of riding was excellent and extensive, because she then did a reverse cowgirl and leaned forward almost having her breast on my knees. Oh please baby, I must admit you have some amazing skills. After a few more jolts of her pussy popping on me I again was threw, and done. She took that power from me again and I was not upset in the least. After the fun, we talked and I asked why you turned me down so much, she replied with this. It was brought to her attention that I might be a LIAR because an ex-girlfriend that went to our gym was spreading hate even tried to say I was FAKE. But come to find out she was upset and just mad because I broke it off once I found out she was married. Damn, she tried to call my LOYALTY into question. She said she wanted to find out for herself so she did. She hugged me as I left and said sex never felt better and it was because I came in and captured her mind. I smiled, said next time I'm keeping control, and her body will belong to me. Now let me swim in your mind even more next time, if you can handle that cubed vision that I have in store. Walking away as she smiled and closed that door, but not the door to her mind.

Pressed

Damn, you just got me feening thinking about how to have you right here and now, u catch my meaning. I want to spread the news that you got me hooked and dreaming. Fantasies about us in many different situations from my mind are a brimming. Good things can only happen when you with me and I with you. Omg, if you only knew a fraction of what I have planned for you.

I'm pressed and only seek to impress, you!

Words can't express the way I feel for you. The way I seek to hold and kiss every inch of you. Capturing my mind's eye and filling all my sight. Chasing you is going to take all my mental might sex appeal to the max and never in doubt. You are the reason I'm writing this, just trying a new route.

I'm pressed and only seek to impress, you!

Now some may think I'm foolish and some may call me crazy. But here I am just seeking to one day call you my one true lady. Oh baby, you came in and set ablaze my heart to burn like a raging fire. Now there should be no reason why you're not all I desire. You are the sunshine in my world. Now forever more you will be my baby, my girl.

I'm pressed and only seek to impress, you!

Those curves I pursue to hug like a nascar racer. I'm coming after you because baby you are my favorite flavor. Drink your juice from that womanly well. Just licking and sucking to make that clitoris swell. So cute and phat makes me want use this black bat. Your mind first, then it's your body I plan to attack.

I'm pressed and only seek to impress, you!

Moving slow and then picking up speed to go in and back
out. Up then down and circles going to have you
completely turned out. Starting out from the back and
kissing you from head to toe. As my hands are exploring
touring wondering where this could go. Now I'm pressed
like I press you to wall. Only mission is to please you so
one day you might just fall.

I'm pressed and only seek to impress, you!

Take all I got and make it all yours. The goal is to show that
this opportunity is knocking at the door. From every image
of you that one can see. It's made crystal that no other man
will be better than me. Now I know I have options and
alternatives but I'm trying to woo you with something more
imaginative.

I'm pressed and only seek to impress, you!

With all this and that said. Has my point reached you,
soaked into your head? I'm just pressed; with a slight twist
of obsessed. So the question remains, are you now
impressed by this piece I call Pressed?

Hero to Zero

I reckon you aren't familiar with this here kind of story. But just maybe you are so this won't sound to shocking to some of y'all. The story is about making every attempt to be the love hero. Not some captain trying to save some hoes, but working and doing everything to be that one to make you believe in love again. As I make every effort to be Robin Hood. Stealing your love and joy from the dark side known as pain. Rescuing that smile that was taken away that is now upside down to be a permanent frown. Want only to be the one to defeat the bad and the evil that entered your world and took your heart hostage, walls that are begging to be torn down.

But this is what happens when a hero is needed to save day for love then all of sudden that knife of destruction is jabbed straight in through the back piercing the heart like nothing else had before. That optimism was just murdered in cold blood. Cold blooded snake just robbed the joy that was building and starting to pick you and gain momentum. The fantasy was where the hero resided but in all actuality the reality of the situation was and is the hero was just a chump, a love torn fool that is just a zero.

This is the story of one who believed they could spread love to all who deserved the best. It's too bad that hero had to go out the way that they did. Just full of hope and love to be that one to share the world with. This story is now over and to that hero there is no hope, not even looking forward to tomorrow, because love don't exist for a straight loser but yet a plain old zero. Not even worth the words to even tell this losers story. But someone has to warn those others wanting to be a love hero. Take the advice from one who knows you can only be a zero because bad and evil are present more in the hearts than love is.

Lynn's Crossing

Thinking about a certain pretty place that one could be that would ensure pure joy and sublime feelings of bliss. Where fun is had by only a select few times that a cheering is needed at this spot you can find it. Prized and sought after, but not easily found. However, if caught at the right time the flow from that secret waterfall will be so warm that you could just dive and just let the cascading affect that is near orgasmic proportions will leave one feeling ecstatic. This sweet locale is located in a hidden away spot known only in mystery that is kept in secret. For those who are lucky enough to pierce the veil to the inner chamber can find immense passionate sensations at hideaway known as Lynn's crossing.

Lies

Building bridges to nowhere with these tools meant for the fool will get you only to one place real fast. I need about three weeks of recovery from the lies. No need to hide or speak falsehood out your mouth. That is one thing that will cause me to be gone. Even a small lie that you think won't go too far seems to last oh so long. Hope is great and optimism is grand that is how I live, but some try to tear all that down with a fib. Fables are told to impart some wisdom and drop some tidbit of knowledge, however that gets twisted, turned upside down and bent all out of shape, hell truth just go out the window and right off the ledge. Temptations are a group that had a lot of hits, but the temptations you gave into just caused you to start some bullshit.

The truth may hurt, but that pain is temporary and though it comes off hard it's real. Lies come off as easy and seem to make coping simple but it's a one sided losing deal. It feels good to you don't it, and gives a feeling of euphoria. After the truth hits, every time I see you it causes a severe case of nausea. Let me see if they worth it to you. I'm talking about the lies you do. Since day one it's been taught to never do such things, however that moral was lost on many out here me thinks. Lies come to separate us, and tear down what was strongly built. The truth might not be provocative but lies carry a whack ass tilt. One day you say one thing and the next it's the complete opposite. That is as pure of a definition of a liar and guaranteed to bring my life no type of profit. So I'm walking out the scene watch the mic as I DROP IT.

"Heartbreak"

When is it time to step back. When is it time to let go.
When is it time to stop playing hard to get. I thought it was
a look or a glance but I'm only getting a negative stance, so
I'm taking it as if I have no chance.

Thinking if you change your ways, you would and could
get further. Somehow you always go away further. Now it
was a time that sharing was caring but I'm not worth
sharing if I'm not worth caring for.

When you feel like a second class person or not worth the
time to know, that just means it's time to go. Preaching and
teaching that all should be respected but in the long run you
are the one neglected.

Is it wrong to desire to have one share your bed for a life
instead of just one night. Does that even sound possible or
even right, just not sure how much longer I can fight.
Provide my eyes with a beautiful sight.

Walking away will take all my might. So let's just call this
our last night. Seeking more and not getting don't sit right.
So you hold on to your other and I will just go seek to
discover my one true lover, the one who wants one and no
other. So I'm stepping back and stepping off, no one's fault
just counts as time loss.

Moonlight

Soft kisses on that moonlit night, standing there eyes meeting, hands intertwined and a feeling between us getting stronger. This adventure is about to get longer than any other. Thought I had it all figured out before but with each gentle touch I desire more. When you look at me, I just want you to see. With you, there is nowhere I would rather be.

This may sound wild and some might call it crazy. But you got me floating so high when you call me your baby. Aint a good day without you, so we stuck here together, nothing no one can do. Igniting a fire deep in me, passion burning bright as the eye can see. After seeing that beauty you possessed when earlier eyes lay upon your beauty.

 I knew it was my duty to please that booty. Meeting up, it was no doubt on what was going to be forced out. With a tongue that moved at varying speeds that caused even the deepest sensations to rise up higher than all 7 seas. Night for some brings thought of closure and an end to a day, but baby I'm telling you it's the start to our special time, what more is there to say.

With legs parted and wrapping around the head, some freaking awesome sounds crept from your lips while you were delivered some superb head in my big ole bed. Heat as we shared each other's flames that burned out of control. Swimming through your mind I enter your body. Touching the inner most places to cause a force to erupt inside you. Only to be repeated over and over again until full sensory overload is obtained.

Tell me have you seen the light from the moon that glows so bright. Well after this night and any warm night that follows, the glow from you will be brighter than any full moon light. Unpredictable are my actions but deliberate are my true intentions. So let me bring you to the verge of sensual insanity only to drive that point deranged romance home. My missile tracked down your homing beacon. Devastating all in its path walls fell and crumbled. Dams broke from the pressure and subsequent gushing, rushing and flowing of moisture soaked as if one fell into an ocean.

Can't stop loving all over you that I don't want to do. I'm being controlled by this pussy which is just too good and tasty. Downtown is where I tend to spend all my time on you. Just think of this moonlight as sign of what we may do. Now we find ourselves standing here, lost in the moment that refuses to end. Building on that wish, this was made on a falling star. Now this excitement you brought to me is always near and never far, a little low key approach to a dream. That can come true for me and you. Forever and ever if we release our hearts from all past hurts.

 So baby I'm yours and yours alone, surrendering myself and my love to you. With the pressing of our lips the deal was done. Lucky to be here in your arms to protect you from all harm this I vow on this night underneath this romantic moonlight.

Ice Run

Unlike any woman I met before, she had the body that
commanded a certain kind of respect when she would walk
in a room. Now I know that the things that crisscrossed
through my mind were just not appropriate because she was
my best friend's wife. But I can't be crucified for thoughts
right, well I don't think you can. But the things this woman
made my mind come up with were serious and intense.

One time, I can remember we were over their house for a
cookout; it was an annual event for the fraternity. Well
needless to say my eyes betrayed me and I think she caught
me starring at her. That normally would not be an issue but
I was looking hungry like a wolf, you know what I mean,
as if she was that lost lamb and I just had to devour her.
Truly, I wanted to devour some parts of her.

 She had on this sexy black and green sundress, with these
sexy strappy flat sandals. I could only imagine how
SWEET her nectar would be as it trickled from her
womanhood into my waiting mouth. I was caught; I just
knew it by the look of shock on her face. Although, it
wasn't a negative type of shock, more like a surprised form
of it. A slight smirk ran across my face like yeah, I was
looking, you caught me. So the rest of the time, I just did
my best to avoid her until the ice ran out.

My frat brother was doing his grill master thing, so his wife
volunteered me to take her to get some more. Never letting
anyone know my thoughts, I was safe that he didn't know,
but she sort of had an idea after the earlier situation. Oh,
well anyway we got in my truck and we drove to the store.
Well they live sort off the beaten path, hence why we
always have the cookout at their spot so we wouldn't have
to worry about nosey neighbors. So driving down this dirt

road to get the main road, it begun, I was hit with the question. So how long have you had a crush on me? Hit with shock, I played it off saying what you mean, not me, you married my dear. She replied back with what the fuck ever, I saw how you were looking at me, and I'm just thinking back now to other times, I caught you looking at me.

Don't even try to deny it. Don't worry, I won't tell, it's our secret. I laughed and smiled and said ok, you right I do, I do. With that said, she was like ok, now we can move on. Feeling a sense relief, I felt more relaxed, and then suddenly her hand was steadily moving up my thigh. Lost focus for a second and asked what you are doing. She said you aren't the only one with a secret crush. But, but, but and before I could get my words out she had me out and in her hand.

Hmmmm that looks so TASTY, LUV to see just how delicious it was, so she went down on me right there in the truck. Damn, I almost ran into the ditch, but I caught enough composure in time to correct it. But we pulled over into this little cutoff and back far enough so no others could spot us. She was going full call of duty on me now, just taking all of me deep inside, long slow slurps up and back down, she was truly making love with her mouth and luckily I was sitting down because I couldn't stand if I could. Speeding up slightly while she gripped firmly, the moisture from her mouth had trickled down and she was using it as lube to stroke me off along with her mouth.

Come on papi, let me have it don't fight me just let go. My eyes were rolling back, I was holding tight to the wheel so I was holding it at 10 & 2. Now that was funny. She said that is it, you going to give this to me now, and I think I blacked out, something she did with some sort of VIBRATIONS with her tongue against that one vein. Hands moving up and down like a jackhammer, mouth acting sucking like a Dyson vacuum as she coaxed that juice out of me. She swallowed all of me not missing a single drop. She said she liked feeling the pulsation of me in her mouth while the eruption shot down her throat. Finally returning to the upright position, and me coming back from my blissed filled daze, she informed me that this was just round one. So let's go get the ice and get back.

Once the party ends, then our fun can resume. Looking at her with amazement for her type of reckless abandon, I said ok because I have been fantasizing about tasting you for a minute. Smiling, she said good, because I been dying to feed you and feel you not just in my mouth, if you know what I mean. So pulling back onto the main road, we continued on to the appointed task. Oh baby, I can't wait till later I thought to myself.

Ice Cold

Getting back to the party and playing things real cool, we walked in with the ice and just went back to partying it up. However know since the ice had been broken between us, she was working her magic like never before. She was real cool with it too, slight little glances here and there, the occasional brushes up against me when she was passing by. Thinking damn, if this woman doesn't stop someone may see or catch on. Hell I was hoping no one saw how she was making me rise up down south. Oh if she only knew how I was going to tear that ass up later. She was TEMPTATION personified; I had to run off to the bathroom once or twice to just calm myself down, which meant I had to get out of her presence.

My mind was betraying and causing my body to do the same. I stayed cool though, even when I was around my frat brother. I knew it would have been devastating if he found out. But I had to go with my urges, and though it was bad, she made me feel so good. The party went into the wee hours and it was rocking the whole time, folks drinking, had all the line dancing going on, you know the booty call, the cupid shuffle, the cha-cha slide, and all the good ole songs. The DJ was rocking and the food was always on point. Just like these joints always turn out to be jamming.

It was bout 2a.m when the last of the folk who stayed was found to be passed out and the others managed to get off to their homes. My frat brother was passed out in his bedroom, so you know what that meant. I and she went off into the woods with a blanket to find this clearing, oh and we brought a bucket of ice, just to keep things a little cool. Once we reached the landing zone, I immediately went and took control of this situation and came up behind her and wrapped her arms around her waist as I placed kisses on her neck and started moving down. As I did, her sundress went down to the blanket as well. Not long though, I followed tracing her body, not missing any curve or lines until I was on my knees and tasting her nectar that was sweet as honey wine. Her lips let out a slight soft HUM, as she began to feel the cool rush shoot up through her body. Little did she know, I had slipped a piece if ice in my mouth before she entered my mouth. Standing there shaking and shivering, not from the cold but rather the heat we were beginning to create originating from her beautifully maintained womanhood.

Taking my time because we were in no rush, licking up and down slow and softly making sure to incorporate that sexy piercing she had that I did not know she had. Taking my tongue to roll around her clit; working that area like I was being paid to be there in her SENSUAL area. I used my tongue to penetrate the front and make circles around the back. This drove her wild, she sighed, moaned and panted repeatedly until that climatic release was obtained. Overcome now with orgasmic bliss, it was time to take this up a level. She then frantically began to undress me until I too was standing in front of her in my full glory with my manhood fully alert and ready to go on a deep mission of exploration.

Just as she slid down to once again briefly taste me, the sky opened up and poured a torrential downpour onto us. This however did not stop the action, no rain delay was needed. She continued to swallow me whole until I felt like a lump of coal just became a diamond and was harder than steel. Rain pouring down and hit our flesh just intensified the sensations we were causing each other to have. She now just the right moment to take me from her mouth as she did, she laid on the now soaked blanket, as I parted those creamy thick and luscious thighs so I could penetrate her middle. Slow and steady to start off, with eyes locked just stoked the fires of desire even more as each stroke became more powerful. Coupled with her drop dead sex appeal, sexy body and now the raindrops just falling to her body just made this more wonderful. Hitting her breast and running down her nipples, I just leaned in to drink of the natural water from the heavens rolling down her frame.

Saying to her, baby this is perfect fulfilling two of my fantasies at one time. She looked at me and said yes, I agree, these too are some of mine. That moment she said now turn me over and take this pussy like you have wanted to do since we first met. Being all too happy to oblige, I pulled out, she turned on all fours, I smacked that ass for good measure and I re-inserted myself in her. This time I thought of every time I saw her, every time I thought of her and I did it, I began to fuck her like nobody's business. She threw that ass back only to be met by my stiffness pushing deeper back in her moving in and out with long, quick bursts.

Soon we were moving in sync as we both inched closer and closer to our pleasure brink. She was first to cross that threshold, moaning and sighing saying damn baby, this shit feels good. She did that, and then contracted those walls on me and that was it, she got it all. I exploded like a Hawaiian volcano, blowing my substance all over. Falling down on her back, we both soaked and satisfied we grabbed up the wet articles and ran back to the house. Sneaking back in past all the knocked out folks, she went up to her room to the bathroom and I used the one downstairs. Thinking to myself damn did that just happen. Next morning, as I left, she hugged me, thanked me and whispered, this won't be the last time.

Conversation

Let's begin with just a little conversation, something that
will be long, deep, penetrating and moving. A tale to
perplex you and vex you, leave you wondering what ever
did he just do.
He was there and oh so ready, he moved in with a style that
was just so slow and steady. Explicit he wasn't, but
persistent and blunt he was with no question.

 Just knew what to do because this is what he is best in.
Now that my attention was his I'm not sure what to do next.
He just has a way and swag about him that leaves me quite
so vexed.

 To be or not to be, that was the state I was in after this
conversation. Mind went one way but he definitely went
down south on me. I knew this would be amazing because
he was adamant about his job like a busy lil bee.

Taking his time and putting in the necessary attention to aid
in reaching his desired mission. Moving that tongue like a
cheetah, with speeds that left one dazed and confused. Then
the sounds that were heard would garner only grandiose
cheers and no boos.

Sensations on the rise, moisture levels reaching maximum,
thighs gripped by his powerful hands, back arched and with
a slight gesture from his lips, that was it, my mind went
crazy and my body shook from the sweet space between
my hips.

He was a linguistically tantalizing my femininity with a
passionate energy that smoothly came from his oral cavity.
Sweetness was that end result as the satisfaction just jetted

out like it was uncontrollable, like they say in the street, diarrhea of the mouth.

Well what he did caused me to release from his trip down south. I see now with just a lil conversation and whispering to that right location will always end in a sensual celebration.

Fragile

Years ago there was a song called "what's love got to do
with it" and it was a movie about a trouble to triumph life.
Well, let me pull more of the veil back on my own life
because I'm asking that same question. We are all blessed
with a heart and the gift of love, well what if you share
your gift with another and they truly mistreated it. There is
another saying, "it's a thin line between love and hate", well
there is literally. This sprung forth a movie that had the
brother laid up in the hospital for saying those three words
and not meaning it. Well with me, I mean it when I say it. I
seek to find that real, true, deep, long suffering love.

Now some love is eternal, a gift from the most high above,
but my love is good, just gets abused and used and once
done with or taken for all it is worth, it get thrown away for
another. Why do the broken hearted get treated so badly. It's
like once you get broken, a sign goes up, that says easy
target. Instead it should read fragile, handle with care.

Now in some cases, others turn the hurt from themselves
and direct it on to the next and that is no good, because you
begin a cycle of destruction that gets hard to break. This
day in age, a lot of people don't care too much about their
fellow man; well I'm stuck in an old time where I still do.
Instead of warming things up in a microwave, having that
quickie, or one night ONLY event, I prefer to put things on
the stove, let them warm to, simmer and then boil to a point
that things bubble over and the passion is so intense that it
will last and stand any test that will come.

 They say "only the strong survive" but if you have a fragile
heart and you can stand up to all that come to try to use and
abuse it, then you are stronger than steel. I know you can't
be turned off by the hurt, but it hurts. And being a man is

no force field from pain, nor is it an automatic excuse that we always are the perpetrators neither. I'm not here to bash or play up the victim role neither, just opening up a little more and suppressing the fear a tad bit more to reveal more of my heart fragile as it is.

 I can't fall into the trap of the woman in the situation, freedom on both sides here on out, because sharing is not caring in that scenario. I'm am a hurt person, that has hurt too, but wants most out of this life to hurt no one and no more for myself. Well here is more of me, I'm opening the door bit by bit, no longer hiding or using sex as an avoidance tool. Here that knock at the door, it's me open up and claim your package just know the contents are fragile, so handle with care.

And if you do, I promise to allow you to reign over the land of love we will share together. The bible says "a man that finds a wife, finds a good thing" well I'm hoping that search is over and I have found that true black gold, that diamond in the rough. As you know time makes all these things that we prize and build empires on, so with time can't we build a love empire together.

Cycle of Destruction

When I was a young man I was taught many lessons. Now
some of them did not catch and that is why the pain will not
lessen.

Lessen would be great if I could just learn to watch for
them damn warning signs. Start by cutting off emotions
from the heart and using more of my mind.

Mind has been plagued with images that tend to be false or
just another lame ass mirage. Going back to the thought
that all gold don't glitter, it's just good ass camouflage.

Camouflaging the ratchet gold digger and the user not to
mention the ones in situations. Trying to weed through and
pick the right one really requires faith and patience.

Patience is not my strong point so I end up picking the
same damn ones I seek to avoid. The only reason I settle is
some misguided belief that I'm lonely and need to fill a
void.

Void that is self-imposed, and then again it might be some
form of karma for the fucked up shit I did when I played,
lied, cheated and stole, literally just broke many of hearts.
Now my life seems like a shambles, broken into small, tiny
unrecognizable parts.

Parts that may never be formed ever again unless directed
to do so from the heavens above. So never being the one to
give up, I hold faith to the optimism that one day I may find
that real true love.

Love is beautiful and extremely powerful if the right steps
are taken to make it, oh so excellent. Too bad I have a bad

habit of rushing it and not getting it to work so out the door it goes leaving my heart with yet another dent.

Dent after dent and still more dents, you would think I would learn my lesson to pay attention to the signs like in that song back in the day. But I don't so I continually end up in this vicious, unhealthy cycle of destruction, what more can I really say.

Say this loud and clear, I'm breaking the cycle with this, no more drama, no involved, married or in any sort if situation or radical distances will be accepted. So sorry if I'm harsh, mean or cutting out any possible opportunities, this is for me, so just respect it.

"Phenomenocity"

Sometimes in life, things become overlooked, neglected and just passed on for something perceived to be better. Well this is done to shine that light on that which was passed on. Now just because the exterior may look fine, it's what is hidden down beneath that matter. Take this classic definition of a phenomenal woman and add to her the strength to get over hurt and pain. Add to that the determination to persevere and hold fast to hope that all will be brighter and better. Practicing the art of phenomencity is what she epitomizes. Daunted and bruised by those unworthy and unknowing of your true gift terrible things to handle but you know how to use it as a step onto the next better course destined for your life. It is always a wonderful sight to see you not linger in the dark but continue to let that awesome, no phenomenal light sign. So you my dear are a true master in the art of phenomenocity.

"Quality"

No more one hitter quitter, no more random fucks. I want something special and I don't want any ole thing. Now Jucy J may not say no to ratchet pussy but I sure as hell can. I want that woman that I can bring to church and take out to the club. Make you want to settle down and say good bye to the game. Where is the woman that will be an example to a daughter on pure womanhood? Where is the woman who stands by her man and is his backbone not the knife in his back?

Believes that love is possible and will fight to have it and hold on to it. Who needs a bunch of women when one will suffice? Where is the woman who knows how to balance career with home. Can juggle her family first needs with her needs of her job. Let's watch a football game together. Let's chill on Sunday morning watching Game day. Where are you so we can just make it a Redbox night?

 Just one of those days you got to be alone, well hey, we all need a break. But let's not break the bond. Where can one dynamic woman be that treats her man like a king and in turn can carry the title of queen? Quality always wins over quantity in that with quality, the void is filled. You are the part I have always been looking for. Not that part that completes me because I'm complete and whole. You are that part that makes me better.

That added addition that enhances all the positives and blocks out all the negatives. You are the piece to GOD's master puzzle. You are a bad son of a gun and I'm just really excited because you are nothing but true real fun. We found the parts we been looking for. Hell, I don't need to hope, wish or look anymore. Hear the knocking; it's me, Mr. Opportunity at your door. Now I know the answer to

my question but do you. Are you the quality woman of
virtue spoke of, well is it you.

Quarter

So I see that you have falling from his pocket. That dime piece he had once claimed and prized ever so much. Now you have the beauty he adored from the jump but something has happened that he now won't even buy you lunch. Coming along and seeing that dime had fallen I knew it was my mission to pick you up and turn you into the QUARTER I know you to be. You have a body that looked to be perfectly baked from a most heavenly baker. Crisp and delectable to the eyes and even sweeter to the touch.

You have mouthwatering attributes and desirable qualities that leave one lost and stuck in time like that one song that sticks around in your mind. Every breath that leaves my mouth I just wish to bring you one step closer to my heart. I feel so upset when I feel we must part. The lips you have beckon to me for them to touch mine. Never in life did I ever expect you I would find. Now I may not be the prettiest crayon in the box, but I know I can be really naked emotionally. He may have said things to you that made you question your body design. But I would like to show you why I think you are better than any dime piece, but better known as a quarter piece and that is because you are two times as nice and deserve five times more than you deserve.

You walk in a room and your presence is immediately felt. Your heat burns hotter than sun, just look outside, you made all that snow melt. Power in your hips, grace in your strut, and curves that make one want to examine each one up close and even more personal. I am not writing this to say anything that you don't already know just here to show you an alternative to your current position. There is reason why I cannot let you say good bye. But rather see you as the substantial and exceptional woman that has star power that reaches sky high. When I think of you all I can say is that I am just here trying to reach up to you. I'm a BIG MAN, so give this big man sum room. Face down and ass up is literally your favorite way, I do pay close attention to what you say. Body pressed to the wall, kissing your body and hitting each spot, one and all. Placed in bed, neck kissed, nipples sucked, baby I undress you because we going to fuck.

Thighs wide and feet on shoulders, dick pressed deep all up inside. Tongue on overdrive, with arms and legs pinned down at your side. Moans in pleasure and you ride like a true champ. You had me flying high like I just jumped off a ramp. Now full of passion for you like a raging fire is this a recap or just something I fully desire? Knowing that you have caused these sensations and looking for a lot more is the mission one has chosen to endure. I need you like never before you put such wonder and mystique in my world. So what must one do to make sure you believe you are two times as nice and worth five times as more?

Poquito Mas

Saw her picture and knew it was her that I wanted. Just a little more of her time was what is desired beauty that belonged on a magazine cover. Women like her are hard to come by for the average guy. Body built like a well-defined machine and that was about it. Just the thought of her makes my mind go just a little hay wired. After meeting her, it was a done deal, no longer wanted another. Now just have to figure out if a little more is done can I get someone so fly. Now she is dope, with a stride looking like she floats. When you look at her, be warned, she so hot her lusciousness will have you melting at that exact spot.

Who knows, a little more time, would just be what it takes to make someone like her mine. Saying it loud and proud that she is the definition of beauty in flawless perfection, even looking at the mirror is jealous of her reflection. Now brick house is a title that could be used too just never met women that fine have you? Mind is working overdrive to find a way to get her attention might just take my time and shower her with praise and a little more affection.

She is hotter than a summer day, springing forth thoughts that leave one feeling a certain way. Cooler than a winter night, falling for her is not only possible but will be oh so right. Being the type of woman she is, it's not mucho mas, but poquito mas that will get her drafted to make this a winning team. Just goes to show that a little goes a long way, know what I mean.

"Questions"

I sit here asking myself some question and I wonder will
they ever get answered? Is chivalry dead, because I find it
in my nature to open doors, pull out a chair? Compliment a
beautiful woman and treat when you go out on a date. Has
the independent spirit killed the chivalrous man? Why can't
a man just want to see a woman treated as a queen? Why
when a man works hard it's seen as a negative thing but
seems more accepted to sit home and play video games or
watch videos all day. Not content with being more in life.
I'm not content to being a dad but more like a father.

Why does being sensitive and showing his softer side
relegate one to a punk status. How about if he can hold his
own in an Ultimate Fighting match but sheds tears at
certain times. Is he still less of a man. Seeing someone cuss
you out and hit you and treat u lesser than a lady is
accepted. Well if you like the thug then this guy is lacking
in that mentality. I'm bringing kuntry passion not thug
passion. I just want to see you smile. The smile that is
brighter than the sun that lights up my world, the world that
I would like for u to share. So like Mary said come share
my world. Why would u not want to?

Regret

Never being one to ever look back on life and feel like any choices made were the wrong ones, this point in life I am realizing that maybe some were. Never would ever regret my children but maybe just made different choices on who I would have partnered with to create them. Even still can one say that too, because if the partner was different would that not make the children here today be different. Would the experiences with them be different and would those choices that were derived would shape some other outcome.

Not really sure what my mind is doing right now. I just know that this trip is waking up my feelings of regret and remorse. When is it ever good to doubt one's choices, I mean life being what we make it, you get knocked down you get back up right. Well what if I made other moves that resulted in me not being knocked down. Well not knocked down as hard as I have. Then I see the children of today who go through life like they are indestructible, was I of that mindset when I was growing up. I just know that this time is allowing me to think and be retrospective on choices that were made.

 Some made out of necessity, some out of hedonistic wants and others because I just thought it was right and true at the time. Either way regret is making a decision and feeling bad that the decision was made. Maybe I'm not in regret mode, just desiring to make better choices that will go against my normal grain and will result in some better outcomes. One never knows what others may see so I'm putting myself out on display.

If knowing me is to love me, then what do you know that makes you love me. Love is powerful and love is true. My biggest life question is do I regret not really knowing love. Or did I have real love and let it go. This is true, that when love does reveal itself to me again, it will not get away no more. Regret for the past is no true answer, learning from it is, then building from it or helping others build off it is the one powerful skeleton key to open up any and every door life has. Now regret, get thee behind!

"Sister 2 Sister"

From the first day, I knew we would be a team unlike any other before. Family is not just a blood tie or some legal piece of paper, but rather bond forged by love from that blacksmith up above. Now there were times when frustration, anger and some petty jealousy stepped in but because sisters go through this, and overcome, just show how strong we actually are. All my love is for you and will always be. The life we have together is such a sight to see. From all the time we spent growing up, all the bumps and bruises, girl talks and boy chasing will be things that I will cherish forever. Love like ours is something that will fade never. Picking on one another, teasing one another and even telling on one another is just part of sibling growth process.

Just knowing we can look back on all that with heartfelt love just aided in making our sisterhood progress. As I read this it may become apparent that I speaking to you as if you are right here. Well that is because you are. A bond and a love this strong no matter what, you will never be too far. Now I know that this is all in his plan and he knows you were ready for a rest. So I only want to thank GOD for giving me a sister like you, it made me feel truly blessed. Now as I say good bye to your earthly form, Sis go up there and keep my spot warm. I know one day we will meet again until then the joys, the pains, the ups and downs we shared, in my heart I will contain with-in. So I will weep no more and let joy return to its reign. You are happy, missed, loved forever, but mostly there is no more pain. So from one sister to another, know that I will always love ya.

Temporary Fix

Do I look like the Band-Aid you would put on a gunshot
called your life? And you ask yourself why I have no wife.
Well this is just a brief piece to let you I am getting out this
ratchet selfish mix. I am not your temporary fix. I am more
than second place and deserve nothing less than to be in the
top place.

Temporary Fix I am not, at least no more.

Talking to you only when you can find that special time
wait more like that secret time. Only when you need that
spot warmed or passionately touched. Sometimes it seems
like this life brings stress way too much.

Temporary Fix I am not, at least no more.

When we get together I will lick you low to move up high,
with hands massaging inner and outer thighs. Seeing the
look of pleasure fall all over your face no wonder I used my
tongue in that special place. Sounds of slurping fill the
room all the time, you get so loud your moans can be heard
in far off space.

Temporary Fix I am not, at least no more.

Finding out the spots to make the heat that you say you
miss, starting out with sensual touches and lips burning
skin from those strategically placed kisses. Shivers raced
up and down your spine to make your knees weak and body
shake only to make that sexual beast in you to wake. The
system to which has be engaged is taking your mind over to
free you like a bird just sprung from a cage.

Temporary Fix I am not, at least no more.

Take my member to enter a club, too bad it's not exclusive like I would I love, but hey the carpet was rolled out for me to plainly see. Hell that spot got extra wet, wetter than any sea. Stroke by stroke, push in and pull out, faster and faster, then back to slow speed made this feel real good to me. Slaps to your ass and maybe a slight choke, hard you released, squirted even from my powerful poke.

Temporary Fix I am not, at least no more.

Now I may have put myself in this position a time or two, hell maybe three or four and still a few more. But like a Band-Aid to a bullet wound this cannot last too long. A quick fix is never enough but maybe when you need that sense of rush, just remember to stay quiet, keep that shit on the hush. So check this out, and I will not be put here in this spot anymore. I like the rough, sensual, hot passionate heat we cause when I spark that dormant fire that he won't anymore. Permanent is what I'm seeking and desire, this temp agency does no more new hires. Just remember the line that has been said earlier before.

Temporary Fix I am not, at least no more, so good bye, watch me turn and leave forever out that door.

Tired

Tired of walking around solo
 Tired of feeling so low
Tired of being used
Tired of getting abused
Tired of the hurt and pain
Tired of my tears falling like rain
Tired of not living out my dream
Tired of not having that special team
Tired of losing the true love I thought
Tired of feelings of distraught
Tired of finding the false and fake
Tired of the liars who just take and take
Tired of being tired, rolled on and worn down like some used up tires
 What does one have to do to finally get fulfilled all their desires
Until that question is answered, tired is who and what I will be. I'm just a country boy, and that takes some getting used to.

Deep

Deep is where the feelings reside and hide. Then you dug down real far to bring this up to the surface like a rising tide. Floating along on dream, hoping one day we might have been the new dream team. Everything in life takes work, and as much as I tried to keep my feelings pressed down, shaken together, I never let them run over. Found myself here once again and not quite sure how I did neither. Deep is the emotions you have me feeling now.

Break taking and leaving speechless, my own moment of wow. Looking forward to each and every moment with you is a joy and a pleasure, thinking you were my never ending treasure. Spirits on sky high mode can't nothing bring me down. That was until all the contradictory SHIT I soon found. Size one, size two, and size three, none of them panties for DAMN sure aint fitting me. So don't lie, tell the truth, you really were never mine, if that was true please explain the earrings I just discovered on my next unexpected find. Now I'm feeling low and hurt by your numerous and unending lies.

Here I thought you were different so that was the reason, a chance was given, better yet a reasonable try. Stepped out on faith, spent my nights with you to build something so true, but OMG you did you and FUCKED it up with some random ASS screw. Not a lot was invested and AMEN for that, and luckily I aint catch nothing because if I did, I would catch a case for beating your ASS with a baseball bat. All from that FUCKING around your RATCHET ASS did. More and more hurt you causing even when I see your name. Yes these tears that fall and the anger that rages and the hurt that encompasses it all, it's because you are solely to blame.

Finally got to the mind that point where I wasn't going to let those that practice the art of bullshit and those that participate in the furthering of lies to exist in my orbit. Let's see I'm not going to say you broke my heart but you bruised it severely just glad I found out early before I truly got bogged down in your BULLSHIT, now it's time to set you adrift on that bad memory ship. Hurt me deep down that you did, but caught myself before I bought in with a life bid. Hurt is dispersed now anger brews up and vent I must do. Why did you think I was just another hit off chick to join your long list of boos? So with all that said I bid you a farewell and take my final words hide them in your soul, down real deep. You cheating, ratchet ASS Negro, you reap what you sow.

Directions

Let's take a trip and slip on dream. Fantasy and wonder, oh what a magnificent team sexual wonderment along with sensual excitement. Four corners of the globe are what is expected, but in a mind like this, just wait for the unexpected twist. Not an ordinary one like from a lime or a lemon, but let's use the cardinal points to please a grown and sexy woman.

North,
This is where all must begin, by reaching in and touching the mind. Smooth out the nuances, stroke the impulses, and massage the synapse to get that perfect desired mental stimulation that brings forth total body relaxation. Ease away all worry, stress, doubt and fear nothing going on in here but the building of a sensual atmosphere. Feel the penetration from the oral distribution of the verbal accumulation of stimulating expression in this simple presentation. Bridging the gap only to expand the space to which will soon be occupied by my face is the goal, so please excuse my varying pace. So open please, so I can insert my toll while on my knees. Tasting, licking and in hopes of sticking, just let your mind wander to the place where fantasy begets reality and springs forth, the mind is set at true north.

South
Down below is the place this will go stepping to you with a look like I was going to devour you fully and whole. Now it's time to go have some fun with the tool that is shaped like the number one. Grabbing hold of those thighs that have me floating sky high curves that bend and wind and leave me lost and hoping to make all you all mine. Body built to my every specification, with no deterring from the original design and no modification. It was the focus to

make you feel so special down south, bet you would like to know what I got planned for you with my mouth. If it was possible to move the tongue in slow motion would that causes your body to produce its own lotion later pouring into my mouth like a sweet love potion. Your scent has me feeling delirious, not too strong but its causing my oral pressure to go fast and furious. Up, to the left, down to the right, back to center are just some ways I maneuver round that swelling clitoris. If you could see how you look right now while my mouth explores your region down south.

East
Turning to the right, moving to that backside is the best side. Hand to ass over and over again to leave a lasting impression. Just think how it will feel once there is full insertion from a deep penetration. Oh what night or day that could be, when that spot is open and receiving all that beef or thick meat. Can't believe it, you throw it back all up on it. Grinding, moaning and bouncing like you on some pimped out ride with hydraulics. Just think this was made possible because you received all those earlier licks. Now the gates are open and all the juices are flowing from so many sticks. Long and slow, deep in and back out is the route this is going. Still had that little man inside you still growing, so this session really was sexually mind blowing. Bet you never knew you had a freaky sex beast hitting you from the back from the east.

West
Facing forward this is the direction that I love the best, it's the breast and I'm a fan of a nice soft chest. Hands moving tracing and touching every inch. Squeezing and kissing, slight nibbles even a gentle pinch. Hands hate being unemployed, they love to work. Just lightly caressing and cupping that just caused them nipples to perk. Closing my eyes to draw a mental picture; starting from the crown of

your head, moving down to run my fingers across your lips, to feel the plumpness, so thick indeed. Excuse my hands as they run across your shoulders, moving further down to give shockwaves that shot through you was exactly what you needed. Your body is like a candy store, with each touch, stroke, glance and kiss just makes one want more and more. Finding you in the darkest of nights or the brightest of days is why each and every time that spell is cast. This is why it's called the wild, Wild West.

This is one sexy compass that leads to a pot of gold at the end of this journey the secret of the well upon which has bewildered many. But there is no map to truly lead you, believe me it's been tried many times. So check this as this is closed out, if you treat a woman like a prize, highly sought after treasure, it's almost guaranteed you will provide her with some extreme pleasure.

Fun with Ice

I want you to gently place you on my lips as we come together to form such a beautiful kiss. Then take your tongue and run it down to my breast and circle my nipples and watch them grow. I then want you to slide your tongue down my body biting my skin gently to feel me squirm from your touch, teasing and seducing me also. I want you to play around my inner thigh just enough I can feel your warm breath on my clit. Watching my juices slowly roll from anticipation of you tasting it. Slide your hands around my thighs holding me from trying to run away when you taste my inner candy. Get a strong hold of my body cause if it's great, I'm running. Nowhere to run and no need to hide moving up and down my body is one sweet ride. Dimensions of perfection got your mind's eye on me and I can see you standing at full attention with some sort of erection hoping it's aimed in my direction. Just the thought of you taking complete control of me and pleasing every spot, inch and corner of my body sends chills throughout. Sensations of pleasure echo in my mind as I can feel my breast firm and nipples protrude, telling you to fuck me with all you got, does that sound rude. Now I know it's your prerogative, but this does matter, I dreamt that I came over and when you let me in you closed the door and pushed my back against the wall and began kissing and sucking my neck. I have a feeling that when it's time to play with ice, I won't have any sort of delay, nope not a single rain check. Melting away at my walls and chipping them with his ice pick is something I truly desire, friction, brings heat and heat brings passion. Who would of thought Ice could cause a wildfire, guess that's why, he is considered a skilled craftsman. Such wonderful things float around in my head when I think of the fun I can have with Ice and his unique and pleasurable device.
"Toe Game"

Sitting at the nail shop, I just think of what could happen while you are getting your toes done. Now you might think why wouldn't I take you home and I give you a sensual foot bath and massage. However, I want to get it professionally done. As I sit next to you in the chair and watch your feet get pedicured and treated royally my mind begins to go on a sensational sensual sabbatical. Just how they raise each foot from the water I think how I would raise each foot to my lips. Begin to kiss, lick and suck each toe with sensual precision. As they clip and scrape the unwanted away from the toe, I can only picture that finally polished toe peeking out of sum sexy peep toe heels that will be wrapped around my head while I make sweet passionate kisses to your yoni. The pink and green cream comes out to mix on your legs to scrub away all the dead skin so that as I'm pampering your toes with my oral skills. My hands travel up your smooth as silk legs as if they traveled down a freshly laid highway. Just this highway leads to the sweet, warm yoni that yearns to be kissed, caressed and pleased. Lastly as the final polish is applied, that alternating pink and blue, I can only imagine the perfect pair of shoes I saw at the store that would go extremely well with the lingerie I picked out for you. Oh wait, that was supposed to be my surprise for you. Well just know your toes are my kryptonite and the sexier they are the more you get from me. I plan to put you on astronaut status. That means we bout to be astronomical when we get together. My eyes have seen this wonderful process of foot pleasure that sent my mind on a journey. This can and will happen every two weeks. Now after all that, we get home. Now you saw this as any regular pedicure, but this had a turn on affect for me and now you my dear will reap all of those benefits. I just want to be the pleaser that had to make all your sexual fantasies come together. Lying on your back and as my tongue probes your yoni; you moan and sigh as to not let me know your true feelings. That orgasm is rapidly approaching, head bobbing up and down as if I was a bobble head doll. Your thighs tighten and as your muscles contract on my head, all I can do is continue to lick and lap the juices you begin releasing as you cry out in orgasmic pleasure. Just then I feel my manhood has reached its full potential. And you slide your hands down to ask how can we use this? Hmmmm, I don't know I replied. That moment you pull my pants down and expose my tool. Wrapping both hands around, you proceed to stroke it, saying this is how I want you to start when you first enter my yoni. Then you speed up with the strokes. Again you say do it like this. Speed up, faster and faster. Then you stop, drop to your knees, but just before you inhale my dick, you say now I'm going to let you imagine what my pussy will feel like wrapped on your dick. Inserting my dick in your warm cocoon of oral heaven, you slurp and suck like this is a tootsie pop and you want that delicious inside. Well go for it baby. I place you on your back and slide your thighs apart. Take my rod and slide in slow as suggested steadily picking up the pace. Those same heels still rest by my ears. This image sends a shockwave of passion and intensity thru ought my body and I turn you to your side, straddle one leg and place the other on my shoulder. I feel my stick poking every inch of your insides. My power is ready to be unleashed. I have passion on overload. Ready baby, here I cum! Wow, and this was the effect of your toe game being tight like rubber bands. Hmmm, this is going to happen every two weeks after your pedicure. Are you game, because I'm ready to play? So what else is there to say?

Pampered

Girl you know it's true I just want to pamper you and show you that this love is true. Let me take you to your favorite nail shop so they can massage your hands and your feet. Polish that pops almost as much as your lip gloss. Oh my queen lets go to that designer shoe warehouse and pick out a few pairs of shoes that will have you feeling sexy, feeling comfortable, and then will leave you feeling satisfied because fuck me heels just have some wild effect on me. No pamper day is complete without a trip to the hair salon got to keep the crown looking right, fresh and tight. Now let me take you back to my spot so I can lay my fingers over your body and show you how special your pleasure being pleased is my tip top priority. Tracing each curve and pressing each button that causes it's on reaction. Walking my fingers down your spine, I can almost feel each sensation fire up through your body applying just enough pressure to your neck that almost made you turn to jello. Baby, this is the remix to the simple tease, this is one that will leave feeling satisfied and mellow. Don't try to label what is happening to you, just relax, and let me part your thighs at your knees. Moving in slow with lips so soft just ready to melt away all stress and after this session, you will be begging for another pamper lesson. I can't even eat without signing my name, and I'm signing it in cursive. Only a chosen few can obtain the right to say they had a session of pampering with me, now my focus is directed to you and you alone. But it's not only your body that deserves this treatment, because your mind is just as fine and it too is beautiful in its own respect. So let me take you on a mental voyage that stretches from your inner most desires to bring them forth and ignite them like some raging wildfires. You have all the tools of the trade, that's because your divinely made, fashioned to my every specification that is why you will be pampered and treated like a queen and get all the edification. Now I know I'm a poet, but your poetry in motion and that garners all my unwavering devotion.

Real Estate

Well when you own property that belongs to only you that is owning real estate. When I say that you have huge amounts of my heart that means despite the way things crashed all due to my inactivity, I still have the same love, passion and intensity to be with you and desire to make you happy. Well we were in our situation for a minute and there is no way I can just let those feelings just fall to the wayside. In life we only have few chances at certain things; well the love we have for one another is special and is strong. Momma always says if you love something and set it free, if it returns then it is meant to be. So my heart is part of your inheritance, come claim my love. And tie me down, cover me with your love and share my world with me. You're the best and I love you and all I want to show you. So love come and let's make this love endlessly grow. The deed is signed, sealed and ready to be delivered. So just embrace the sensations that are making you shake and shiver. You're the best and I love you, granted no one can legally own another but you have them special keys to my heart. So use them and get ready for some unchained passion that will never make us part. So once again come claim the love you possess and freely given from me.

"The Watcher"

Coming home from a great romantic dinner I believe was my neighbor and his wife. They were a wild swinging couple. It would be no surprise to see them with another female or another guy or a couple. This time was no different. There was a car parked outside that this beautiful thick chocolate goddess got out of when my neighbors pulled in to their driveway. I thought to myself this is going to be good, I got to go see this. So I crept over to the window and watched. My neighbors Alex and Eb at the dining room table as they poured their friend a drink. Alex then walked over to the lady and began to kiss her neck; Eb pulled out sum hand cuffs and locked her to the chair. Then Eb began to pull out her breast and push them in the girls face. That is when Alex said her name as he shouted suck them pretty nipples Vicki. As she did as she was told, Alex pulled out his dick as Eb began to stroke it, still with her beautiful heaving chest in Vicki's mouth. I was thinking damn I been wishing I could suck on her breast since they moved next door. I felt my dick swelling up as this scene started getting hotter. Alex then moved to sit on the table facing Vicki, with his dick standing at full attention he told her to place her full thick lips on and suck it. Eb then took off Vicki's skirt and ironically she had no panties on. Eb began to lick between her thick thighs reaching her pussy and began to suck on her clit. Vicki became distracted while that hardness was in her mouth. Alex grabbed the back of her head and began to fuck her mouth and saying focus, you better focus. Eb taking breaks said no baby; I'm going to make her cum so get ready. Watching this competition it was coming down to who was going to cum first Vicki or Alex. Damn I wish I was there with them, my dick was throbbing. Vicki came first and hard, and loud as she was gagging on his dick. Shortly Alex exploded as she swallowed all his juice. Eb said I won so that means I get the dick first. As it was the deal Eb climbed on the table and mounted Alex's dick and began to ride like she was in the Kentucky Derby. Vicki still cuffed could only watch. In between moans, he looked to Vicki and said I told you should have focused. Back and forth and up and down Eb took that entire dick, as she reached the apex of satisfaction she fell back and squirted her juice all over, Alex. Releasing Vicki from her restraints, she bent over the table and Alex came in behind her still with a hard dick, he pressed all his meat up into her still soaked pussy. Long slow strokes then speeding up smacking her ass she moaned in pleasure just as Alex was about to cum he pulled out and blasted over her ass. Standing outside this window was good and bad. Good I saw this hot ass live porno bad because I was hard and horny as hell now. Well as the excitement ended, I crept back to my house. Thinking who can I call, what to do, what ever to do. Next thing I know, a knock was at my door. I opened it, and to my surprise it was Vicki. She said she had seen me watching while Eb was riding Alex. She caught a glimpse and asked me did I like the show, and if I needed help putting my dick back down. Before I could answer, she dropped to her knees and pulled out my hardy boy and sucked it like she was the cure. Slurps and slobs echoed thru my front door, I thought to myself, damn she focused now like shit. Knees getting weak I grabbed the door frame, saying baby you bout to get a surprise. She said bring it, and I brought it. She swallowed it all. Getting up from her knees, she said next time just come over and join us. She left and I stood there with my dick out, in amazement. Closing the door, I felt like I just won the super bowl and I was going to Disney World.

"The Nurse"

You ever wonder what would happen if you dated a nurse or doctor. Well I have and it was amazing. Coming to work and no one knowing I was her man. We sneak off to a room in L&D. It's private so no one would disturb us. Plus the bed comes with stirrups. Perfect for when I was ready to apply that tongue pressure to that wet open spot she called her pussy. Closing the door and locking it, I turned her and pressed her to wall began pulling off her scrubs feverously, to expose those green and white thongs with the matching green lace bra. Turning her face to the wall I take my left hand and press to her neck with some pressure, not enough to make her pass out but force to let her know Daddy bout to own her body and force passion out from all her openings. Sliding my other hand to pull that thong off to slip two fingers inside and massage her walls. The moisture was beginning to flow and I felt them juices percolating.

Taking the bra off with my teeth, watching those beautiful mounds of joy break free caused my dick to jump. Thinking in my mind I'm about to suck the life out them nipples. Turning her around and pressing her back to the wall, I raise her left leg, again slide two fingers deep inside her soaked, dripping pussy, I lean down to suck her nipple. Feeling it stiffen in my mouth, I start to flick it and nibble it with my teeth. Switching positions, I raise the other leg, and slide three fingers in this time and repeat the pleasure to the other nipple. After she moaned from pleasure, I then moved her to the bed. Leaned her over the bed and proceeded to eat her pussy from the back. Tongue gliding across all the gushy moisture she had leaked out from my fingers.

Reaching up I pulled her hair and stuck my tongue in her pussy and licked around her ass. I felt the rush of excitement shoot thru her. Standing behind her I knew it was time to unleash the throbbing dick that was in my pants. However she had other plans. She told me lay on the bed; she put my feet in the stirrups and took my dick and devoured it whole. I swear, her mouth was a black hole of passion. I never felt so good before. She climbed on top, placing her pussy in my face and said if you touch it, then she would stop. I kept my hands to my side even as she forced that good nut from my dick straight down her throat. Moments later a knock came to the door. We knew we would have to finish this story later.

Orbit

I love the way you make me feel. I'm thinking about you all the time. It's not even enough hours in a day that my thoughts are not dedicated to you.

On a scale of 1-10, you are a solid 100. You send my heart soaring to new heights that it belongs in its own orbit. Just to float around your soul is my own personal goal.

You have an astronomical beauty that breaks all molds. Your desires all I wish to attract and forever hold. Excuse me if I am just a tad bit bold, but without you my galaxy just seems dark and cold.

Looking to build something extra special that is beyond strong that will never fold.

 So I'm making every attempt to blast off and take the journey to parts unknown. Baby you are the adventure and I plan to explore you and your heart will be my new home.

I need you every day like the sun shines to light the world, you lit up my soul. And like the moon is the guardian of the night, allow me to guard your mind, body and soul as one big beautiful whole.

Up here is where I belong, and you belong by my side, so never worry because I plan on keeping you. Trust me, I'm not going anywhere, I will never leave you.

You exist in mine and I only seek to exist in your personal orbit. If you don't know what I'm talking about, it's our bond that's tighter than a Victorian corset.

Photo Shoot

Never had I experienced a beauty such as hers before. All I knew was that I wanted to immortalize her image in a tastefully done photograph. With that being said I knew it was imperative to schedule her for a special and unique photo shoot. We had been talking about this for a while and I was not sure if she ever took me seriously or not but after that date of the appointment, she will always know how professional I am and how I stand by my word. It had been a few months gone by that I initially asked her about posing for me, but due to her busy schedule and life it was all just bad timing. Now don't get me wrong we talked quite a bit and even made plans to hangout from time to time. This was so good between us that we became friends. So when it was finally time for this shoot she arrived to the hotel room that was set up with candles in the bedroom and in the living room area it was lit with the natural light from the open curtain. When she walked in the room I noticed that she was looking a little sad, so me being the caring individual and friend I was, I asked what was wrong. She explained to me that she was sort of disappointed that she had missed a call from her special friend. I was like oh I know firsthand how that can be especially when you don't see them that often and you have to try to work around their schedule and life situation. Talking to soothe her mind and cracking some jokes that came across as corny put a smile on her face and that smile she had was like sunshine on a very dark, gloomy and cloudy day. Next I informed her that we would do 3 particular shootings, one would be outside, and thinking the natural beauty of the world would be complementary to her natural beauty. Next would be a sexy boudoir shoot, laying in a big four poster bed with satin and lace sheets, all that will hug and accentuate her curves and sensual definition. Finally the last would be a sensual bathroom shoot, a bubble bath that would cover her womanhood just enough that it was still so tasteful where we would move to the shower and have her pressed to the frosty glass to see that sexy shillouette. After gathering up my camera and she put on her make-up along with sexy summer dress that have just enough cleavage that it still embodied classy with a twist of sexy. Now as we walked out the hotel, I informed her that this spot was chosen because it had a nice beautiful park across the street from it where there was a nice playground. So with this bright multicolored dress on, I had her stand next to a tree. Just embrace it, show the tree some love, let it know you appreciate it for giving you oxygen. She giggled and that was what I trying to get her to do, her smile again was enchanting. We then moved to the sliding board, and she sayt on the bottom, with her legs open, hand holding her dress down in the middle between her sexy thick thighs and legs. Leaning forward a bit to expose just a tad bit more of her twins. Dam, thinking to myself this is going to be a tough day for me. I beganto wipe my brow cause her hotness was radiating like a furnace. Moving to the swings where she went back and forth real slow, kicking here legs out, with the dress just flowing slightly enough to show a little more thigh, she had on these cute wedges, and I just snapped away, but this woman was making me feel like an amateur. I kept it up though and took some great shots of her. Although, something made me feel that she was being extra flirty, however I just played it off. Next back to the room, she changed into a nice bra and panty set, black with pink lace and these fishnets and these black with pink heels. Taking candid shots of her walking around the room, laid out across the bed, and even wrapped around one of the post of the bed. Sitting on the side of the bed, she asked if I would like a little show, still that consumate professional, I said go ahead, just don't get naked, this is not that kind of shoot. She grinned and said yes daddy. Hmmm, hearing that I grinned and something went through my mind, but back to business. She started by coming out of the heels, then peeled each thigh high fishnet down only to throw it at me. At that moment I knew she was flirting with me, or maybe for the camera, yeah it was all for the camera, im sure of it. We never crossed those lines. Crawling on the bed with one strap down dangling off her shoulder, she had this look like she was going to devour me, as I told her bring it, this is pure sexyness. I must admit, she was looking so hot, I thought the lens would melt. As I said next, I just still convinced myself this was all for the camera. Stepping from the bedroom and making her way to the bathroom as it was the final site for this shoot. Dropping the bra and let the panties fall as she walked so sensually to the edge of the tub to run the water. As she sat there, dipping one hand into the running water to check the temperature, the other hand covered both breast as her legs sat crossed. The camera loved her, as much as I did, but I digress, this was just about capturing her beauty and sensuality. As I snapped these images, she stood up to expose all her heavenly gifts to me. Dam near dropping the camera I asked what was going on, she said I know you not slow, I been tryin to seduce you all day. So since you can't get the subtle hints, I just decided to be upfront. Now put your camera down and come join me over here for this bath and shower. Snapping back to reality, I realized I was daydreaming, she had slipped into the tub, bubbles covering her fantastic body, raising her hands up and playfully blowing bubbles, I still remained the total professional. I was just about ready to tell her to move to the shower, but she stepped up, stepped out the tub, water dripping and still a lingering of bubbles attached to her body. She reached out, grabbed the camera from me, placed it on the sink and begun to kiss me while she undressed me. Wait, hold up, what are you doing as hastenedly took off my clothes until I too was just as bare as she. Thinking this must be another dream, but she gently bit my lip, an asked do you still think this a dream, immediately I screamed, oh hell no! We moved over to the shower, opened the door, turned on the water and it was like our passion was also turned on. The deep, strong passionate kissing was intense. The embraces were tight and powerful, hell you would think the heat we were generating caused that shower to become a sauna. Hands chasing every drop of water as it ran the course of her body, her lips chased the water as it ran down my body. As the water continued to run, the heat we had just got hotter and hotter, she looked at me and said I can safely say our photo shoot is over. Humbly I agreed and we finished our shower only to move to the bedroom to finish this sensual twist to this shoot. One day, I may have to tell what happened next, until then, im just going to reminisce from the mental pictures of a top model.